THE GISMO TRILOGY

THE GISMO TRILOGY

KEO FELKER LAZARUS

WILDSIDE PRESS

Published by Wildside Press LLC.
www.wildsidebooks.com

THE GISMO

CHAPTER 1

What is it?

When Jerry Cole rode his bike home from Bridgeville Junior High, he pedaled furiously down School Street. At the first corner he thumbed the handlebar shift lever to high, back pedaled a second, and leaned right into Elm Street.

The wind combed his red hair straight back and roared in his ears. He liked to imagine he was the pilot of a jet plane or flying saucer zooming through space at a zillion miles an hour. For one block he pumped rapidly, then leaned into Park Lane, swung out of the bike seat, and rode the pedal up the driveway of the third house on the right.

Jerry arrived home from school every afternoon in exactly seven minutes…every afternoon that is, except Thursdays.

On that day he took his time and rode home slowly by way of the alley that ran for three blocks behind all the important stores in Bridgeville. Thursday afternoons the shopkeepers put the trash out for the early Friday morning collection. Hal's Hobby Shop threw lots of good boxes away, and sometimes broken models from do-it-yourself kits. Gormley's Radio and TV Clinic dumped old radio tubes and capacitors into the foam packing of big television cartons. Jerry always checked through these cartons of trash. You never knew when Mr. Gormley might discard a broken transformer, a few usable lengths of solder, or those tiny plastic boxes certain radio parts came in. Now that Jerry was interested in building radios himself, he could use such items.

This Thursday afternoon Ron Baily, his best friend, rode beside him. Ron, who was in the seventh grade with Jerry, lived next door.

They guided their bikes slowly down the alley, eyeing each trash bin they passed. At Gormley's they squeezed the hand brakes on their bikes, knocked the kickstands down, and began to rummage in the foam packing of a large discarded television carton.

"Wow! Look at this!" Ron exclaimed. "A whole spool of wire! Why would he throw *that* away?"

"Here, let me see." Jerry took the spool. He half closed his blue eyes, and squinted at the spool, turning it over in his hands. He wrinkled his freckled nose. "It's corroded on one side, that's why." He tossed the spool back to Ron.

"So what?" Ron caught the spool and flipped his shaggy black hair from his round face. "I can still use it." He stuffed the spool into his jeans.

Jerry tugged at a length of spaghetti tubing. It popped out of the carton, and he inspected it closely. It was split down one side. He threw it back. "I guess Mr. Gormley hasn't had much business this week…no decent junk," Jerry said and scuffed along the alley in the shadow of the power-line pole that stood behind Hal's Hobby Shop. Next to the pole there was a rusty oil drum stuffed with papers and boxes. In the first box he opened, he found half a plastic Gemini space capsule model. But although he rummaged deep among the papers and boxes, he couldn't find the other half. He threw the plastic back into the trash. "Nothing here, either," he said. "Come on, let's go home."

Jerry flipped the kickstand up on his bike and was about to swing his leg over the seat when out of the corner of his eye he caught a metallic gleam. It came from the weeds along the alley—a spot halfway between the television carton and the metal trash barrel. Jerry leaned his bicycle against the power-line pole, walked over and lifted the tiny metal object from the ground. It was rectangular, the size and shape of a domino. Tiny knobs extended from either end and a third knob from one side. It felt slippery, like a quarter covered with quicksilver, yet it was light as balsa wood. The upper surface was covered with short, silver-colored brush-like wires. Jerry touched them. The wires felt soft and silky as fur.

"Ron! Come here!" Jerry cradled the tiny object in his hand.

Ron dropped a broken television knob back into the trash and loped to Jerry's side. He put his plump hands on his knees and peered closely. "What is it?"

"Search me!" Jerry said. "Maybe it's a modular circuit from a transistor radio." He had heard the older boys in electric shop talking about modular circuits, but he hadn't seen one yet.

Ron shook his head. "Nope, it's not that. Remember when I dropped my transistor radio through the bleachers at the football game last week and it smashed all to pieces?"

"Yeah?"

"Well, it had a modular circuit and nothing like this gismo fell out of it. Say, aren't those wires moving?"

Jerry drew the object away from Ron's face. "You're breathing on them, that's why. Man! I'd sure like to know what this gismo is!"

Ron put his hands in his hip pockets. "Hey! I'll bet it came off one of those remote control planes…like the one in Hal's window."

"Yeah!" Jerry opened his hand and looked at the gismo more closely. He could see no visible seams or screws holding it together.

Ron reached into his pocket. "I'll trade you this spool of wire for it."

Jerry grinned and shook his head. "Nothing doing! I'm keeping it!"

"Why?"

"It's something I can use, that's why!"

Ron mounted his bike. "How can you use it if you don't know what it is?"

Jerry slipped the gismo into his right-hand pocket and climbed on his bike. "Don't worry, I'll find out what it is!"

When he coasted his bike up the driveway, his eight-year-old sister, Dodie, was slamming a rubber kickball against the garage door. The ball bounced back and hit his bike. Jerry reached down and grabbed the ball. He leaned his bike against the maple tree by the front porch, tucked the ball under his arm, and loped around the corner of the house toward the back door.

Dodie flipped her red braids over her shoulders and started after Jerry. "You give that back, Jerry Cole!"

Jerry ran ahead of her keeping just out of reach until he came to the back steps, then he looped the ball over her head. It hit the garage wall with a bang and bounced away onto the front lawn.

Dodie stamped her foot. "Brothers!" she exclaimed, and ran after the ball. Jerry slammed through the back door into the kitchen, fragrant with baking.

"Hi, Mom," he greeted his mother who was taking a pan of cookies from the oven. He closed his eyes and sniffed loudly. "Don't tell me—*peanut butter!* Right?" He opened his eyes.

His mother smiled. "Right!" She handed him a hot cookie on the end of the spatula.

"Thanks." Jerry tossed the cookie back and forth in his hands to cool it, then popped it into his mouth and munched loudly. He wiped his greasy hands on his jeans and felt the gismo in his pocket. He pulled it out. "Ever see a gismo like this, Mom?"

His mother slipped a second pan of cookies in the oven. "What's a gismo?" she asked.

Jerry reached for more cookies. "Oh *you* know! It's a—a gadget, a—a thing!" He stuffed a cookie into his mouth. "Have any idea what this is used for?"

His mother took the gismo and turned it over. "Is it a brush of some kind?"

"Don't think so—not with those knobs on the ends."

Mrs. Cole handed it back. "I'm not a very good guesser, Jerry. Ask Dad when he comes home tonight. He'll probably know."

Jerry stuffed a few more cookies into his pockets, and tossing the gismo into the air, started through the hall. His older sister, Lou, just turned fourteen, lay on her back across the hall runner. She was talking on the telephone. Jerry pretended not to see her and raised his foot as though to step on her stomach.

Lou let out a little screech and grabbed his foot. "Jerry Cole! You stop that!" She gave his leg a twist and threw him off balance. Jerry fell, knocking the telephone out of Lou's hand. The gismo slithered across the floor.

"Hey, Mom!" Jerry yelled, "Who left a rolled-up rug in the hall for people to fall over?"

"You little monster!" Lou exclaimed. She pushed him away and reached for the telephone. "Not you, Linda," she said into the phone, "this stupid brother of mine!"

Jerry got to his knees. "I've lost my gismo."

"Your *what?*" Lou asked.

"Ah, here it is!" Jerry reached behind the leg of the telephone stand. He sat back on his heels and stroked the gismo's silky wires.

Lou sat up. "Is that thing alive?"

"Yeah!" Jerry snaked the gismo along the floor toward Lou.

Lou jumped to her feet. "*Mother-r-r*, Jerry's got a mouse or something in here!"

Mrs. Cole came into the hallway. "That's enough, Jerry," she said sternly. "And Lou, tell Linda good-bye. I want you to set the table for supper."

Jerry stood up and clumped toward the stairs. "Sisters!" he muttered to himself.

After dinner, Jerry brought the gismo into the living room. His father was watching a local newscast about a recent UFO sighting near Bridgeville.

Jerry sat down on the couch beside his father. "Man! I'd sure like to see one of those UFO's close up, wouldn't you, Dad?"

Mr. Cole smiled. "If there's anything to see… They could be optical illusions, ionized air plasmas, or…"

Jerry grinned and leaned back. "…or swamp gas. Yeah, I know." He stuck his hands into his pockets and felt the gismo. He drew it out. "Ever see anything like this before, Dad?"

His father reached over and took the gismo. He turned it over slowly. "No, I haven't, Jerry, what is it?"

"That's what I'd like to know!"

"Where did you get it?"

"I found it near the trash barrel behind Gormley's."

Mr. Cole handed the gismo back. "Why don't you ask Mr. Gormley. If he threw it away, he'd know what it is."

Jerry rolled the gismo in his hand. "It might have come from Hal's Hobby Shop, too. He's right next door to Gormley's."

Mr. Cole rose and switched the television off. "Well, ask Hal, too." He smiled at Jerry. "There's always a logical explanation for things like that. They don't simply fall out of the sky."

"Off that UFO, maybe?" Jerry grinned.

Mr. Cole tousled Jerry's hair. "With an imagination like yours, Son, you're bound to find out what it is!"

CHAPTER 2

A strange voice

The next afternoon Jerry leaned his bike against the maple tree and ran for the back stairs. His trip to the TV Clinic and Hal's Hobby Shop had been fruitless. He scuffed into the kitchen and opened the refrigerator door. He stood looking in.

"Jerry," his mother called from the hall, "close the refrigerator door, please."

"I'm hungry," Jerry called back.

"Then help yourself to apples. And Jerry, did you put your bike away in the garage?"

"I'll do it later, Mom." Jerry reached for two apples, slammed the refrigerator door, and ran upstairs to his room. He kicked the door shut with one foot and plopped down on his bed.

The crystal radio set he had made at school was on his nightstand. His pocket transistor was there too, but it was more fun to fool with the crystal set. Now for some quiet relaxing music, Jerry thought. He placed one apple on the stand, and with the other apple between his teeth, he picked the headphones up and adjusted them over his ears. He checked the aerial that ran behind his bed through the window screen to the top of the maple tree. Yes, it was attached securely. He glanced at the ground wired to the heating duct close by. It was in place, too. Then he reached for the crystal radio and moved the tuner bar across the coil until he heard the voice of a disk jockey on the local radio station.

He leaned his head back on his pillow and crunched into the apple while he listened to the beat of a new tune. He put his hand into his jeans pocket, pulled the gismo out, and rolled it between his fingers and palm. He liked the slippery feel of it. Placing the gismo on the pillow beside him, he turned his head and stared at the tiny knobs on the ends and one side. What had it been attached to, he wondered...

wires?…clips? Did it fit into a slot? Was it a cartridge of some kind? And those fine hair-like wires on top! Were they antennae? He blew on them and they parted like the fur on a cat. Hal had said it might have come from a telephone truck or a lineman's pocket. If so, it could have something to do with a telephone. Maybe it was a relay of some kind, or a new type of transformer.

Jerry took another bite of apple. Funny how grown-ups like Mr. Gormley, and even Hal, gave up so easily. He'd have to figure out the secret of the gismo himself.

Somebody was thumping on his door. "You there, Jerry?" It was Ron.

"Sure, come on in." Jerry took the earphones off.

Ron walked in. "Your mom said it was okay to come up."

Jerry reached for the apple on his night-stand. "Here, catch!" He lobbed the apple at Ron.

Ron caught it as it hit his stomach. "Thanks," he said and bit into the apple. He flopped down on the foot of the bed. "Whatcha doing?"

"Fooling around with the gismo."

"Got any ideas what it is yet?"

"Well, it isn't a TV part."

"How do you know?"

"Gormley said so. Picked up a couple of alligator clips at his store after school."

"Then I'll bet it's a model-airplane motor like I said."

Jerry shook his head. "Hal said it wasn't that, either. He looked it over real good." Jerry picked the gismo up and turned it over in his hand. It doesn't come apart…no screws…no seams…nothing. These knobs on the ends and sides…maybe something was attached to them."

"What, for instance?" Ron leaned back on the bed and munched loudly.

"Electric wires, maybe, like Hal said."

"For what?"

"Oh, anything. It might be a battery of some kind, you know."

"Yeah? How can you tell?"

Jerry sat up. "Remember in electric shop when we learned how batteries worked?"

"Sure, I remember."

"Well, if this gismo is a battery, I could attach wires to the little knobs on it, then touch the wires to a flashlight bulb, and the bulb would light up."

"Okay, let's try it." Ron sat up.

Jerry hurried to his desk, cluttered with bits of wire and parts of old radios. He rummaged about in one of the drawers and found his flashlight. Removing the glass from the front, he unscrewed the tiny bulb. He selected a short wire from his desk and wound one end of it carefully about an end knob on the gismo. The other end of the wire, he wound about the brass threads of the bulb. He found a second wire on his desk and fastened one end to the other end knob on the gismo.

He brought it over to the bed. Ron held the gismo while Jerry carefully touched the free end of the wire to the dot of solder on the flashlight bulb. They looked closely. There was no glimmer of light.

"Maybe if you attached a wire to the side knob it would work," Ron suggested.

Jerry tried this, but still the bulb would not light.

Ron leaned back on one elbow and tossed his apple core into the wastepaper basket across the room. It landed with a loud *thunk*. "Well, it isn't a battery," he said. "Got any other bright ideas?"

Jerry sat with his chin in his hands. "If it doesn't store electricity, maybe it conducts it. Remember when they showed us how a string of Christmas tree lights worked in a series?"

"Sure," Ron said. "If one bulb was loose or burned-out, the whole string wouldn't light."

"Yea, because a loose or burned-out bulb wouldn't conduct electricity." Jerry leaned forward. "Now if we connect this gismo in a series with something else, we can tell if it conducts." He went to his closet. "I've got my dry cell battery for starting model planes in here somewhere." He hunted among the boxes under his clothes and brought out a large, round battery. He carried it to his desk. Reaching into his jeans, he pulled the two alligator clips out.

Ron joined him at the desk with the gismo. Jerry removed the wires from the gismo and the light bulb and carefully attached a clip to each wire. He clamped the wires to the two terminals on top of the battery. The loose end of one wire he fastened to one end knob of the gismo. The loose end of the other wire he wound around the brass threads of the flashlight bulb.

He selected a third wire from his desk and attached one end of it to the other end knob of the gismo. "There!" Jerry put his hands on his hips. "The gismo's in a series." He leaned forward and touched the dot of solder on the light bulb with the free end of the third wire. The bulb didn't light. He tried again.

"Here," Ron said. "Let's try this." He removed the third wire from the end of the gismo and attached it to the side knob, then carefully touched the free end of the third wire to the dot of solder again. The bulb flickered a moment, then glowed softly. "Hey! It works!" Ron exclaimed. "It *does* conduct electricity!"

Jerry snapped his fingers. "Remember Hal said it might have fallen from a telephone truck?"

"Yeah?"

"Well, if it conducts electricity, maybe it conducts other things— like radio waves." He looked about his room. "If we could attach it to..." His eyes lit on the crystal radio set on his nightstand. "Hey! How about this?" Quickly he detached the gismo and hurried to the stand. He loosened the cat's whisker and crystal from the radio and fastened the gismo by its two end knobs in their place. He put the headphones over his ears and moved the tuner bar across the coil. There was a loud hum, but he couldn't tune in any radio stations.

Ron stood beside him. "What do you hear?"

"Nothing...just a hum."

Ron studied the set for a moment, then reached down and changed an end wire to the side knob of the gismo as he had done before.

Jerry jumped. "Wow!"

"What is it?" Ron asked eagerly. "Let me listen, too." He lifted the headphones from Jerry, turned one earphone so it faced outward, then put the set back on Jerry's head. Ron sat down next to Jerry and put his ear to the turned-out earphone. From the sputtering static a voice came in loud and clear. "XR...calling XR...come in, XR." The voice was high-pitched.

"You've got a ham radio band!" Ron exclaimed.

"On a crystal radio set?" Jerry glanced at the gismo, then caught Ron's arm. "Look at the gismo!" The tiny silver wires on top had become a faint pink color.

The voice came again. "XR...please report in." The wires on the gismo glowed cherry red as the voice spoke.

Jerry reached over and gingerly touched the glowing wires.

"Are they hot?" Ron asked.

"No, they feel cool." Jerry answered.

The voice began. "We have had no message from you since you entered the atmosphere of Planet Three, Sun G six zero eight, Syklo Galaxy."

Ron Chuckled. "Syklo Galaxy…that's a good name for a science-fiction program. What station have you got?"

"I don't know." Jerry moved the tuner bar across the coil again, but only the humming came through.

The voice returned and the gismo glowed red. "Can you hear us, XR?" The voice sounded eager. "We're beginning to receive your transmitting signal now. Are you in trouble? We repeat: Are you in trouble?"

"Maybe we've hooked onto an airlines band." Ron said.

Jerry shook his head. "Airports and pilots don't talk about planets."

"This must be a gag of some ham operator," Ron said.

"XR…calling XR…your signal is clear now, but we're receiving no message… Repair craft are waiting for you at crater 7 del 5, natural satellite, Planet Three, Sun G six zero eight, Syklo Galaxy… over."

Jerry frowned. "That doesn't sound like a gag message to me… That sounds like a real one from outer space."

Ron looked at Jerry in surprise. "It's got to be a gag! No one has cracked radio signals from outer space yet, let alone heard them in our own language!"

The gismo glowed as the high-pitched voice broke in again. "XR…we repeat…repair craft are waiting for you at crater 7 del 5, natural satellite Planet Three, Sun G six zero eight, Syklo Galaxy… do you read us?… Over."

Jerry turned, and snapped his fingers. "I *know* this sounds crazy, but maybe it *isn't* a gag!"

"You've got to be kidding!"

"No, I'm not, Ron. Remember when we studied the solar system in Miss Mill's class?"

"Yeah?"

"She said billions of stars circle around in the galaxy we call the Milky Way. Remember the Greek name she used for it? Meant something like 'milky circle of stars,' I think."

Ron wrinkled his forehead. "Galax… *Galaxias Kyklos,* wasn't it?"

"Right! And doesn't that sound like 'Syklo?'"

"Yeah, but…"

"Miss Mills said our star, or sun, is out near the edge of the Galaxy and has nine planets circling around it." Jerry went on eagerly. "Earth is the third planet from our sun. Right?"

"Right."

Jerry leaned forward. "And what's the natural satellite of the earth?"

"The moon, of course," Ron said.

"And remember the report someone brought to school about astronomers seeing strange lights around one of the craters on the moon? And that UFO sighting near Bridgeville the other night?"

"What are you driving at, Jerry?"

"Oh, come on, Ron! Don't you get it?…UFO's…the moon. Earth's natural satellite with strange lights by a crater, maybe crater 7 del 5… The earth… Planet Three… The sun…maybe number G six zero eight, to anyone that's counted all of them…and Syklo that sounds almost like Kyklos, the name for our own Galaxy… Doesn't it add up?"

Ron looked at Jerry. "You mean this message could be for real? But from what?"

Jerry took the headphones off. He gazed at the gismo, then back at Ron. "That gismo didn't come off any old radio or television set. It didn't come from a telephone truck, either." His voice was low. "It came from that spaceship, XR!"

CHAPTER 3

Is that you, XR?

Both boys were quiet for a moment; then Ron stood up. He stared at the crystal set and shook his head. "If that gismo fell from a spaceship, it would still be orbiting out there." He waved his arm toward the window.

"Not if the spaceship wasn't out there orbiting the earth, too," Jerry said.

"But if the gismo entered the earth's atmosphere, it would burn up! You know that." Ron exclaimed.

"Not if it was lost while the spaceship was in the atmosphere," Jerry suggested.

Ron shook his head. "It would be smashed to pieces when it hit the ground…like my transistor radio."

Jerry leaned forward. "Not if it fell off a spaceship that was *on* the ground."

Ron grinned. "Back of Gormley's shop? Ha!"

"Well, maybe they were investigating something."

"Like the trash boxes, maybe?"

"Who knows what they investigate when they land!" Jerry said. "We know they *do* land, and there was a UFO over Bridgeville the other night!"

Ron picked the headphones up and slipped them on. "I've got to hear this thing again to believe it!"

But before Ron had the earphones adjusted, a loud wail of music filled the room. Ron spread his hands and shook his head.

Jerry ran to the door and stuck his head into the hall. "Hey, Lou! Turn your record player down! We can't hear my radio in here."

"Turn your radio up, then," Lou yelled back.

"I can't. It's my crystal radio."

"Tough!" Lou shouted.

"Darn her! Just a minute, Ron, I'll be right back." Jerry started for the door, but Ron stopped him.

"Forget it, Jerry. Unhook the gismo and we'll take it over to my place. I've got my crystal radio set up in the workshop, where it's quiet."

Jerry removed the gismo from the wires and slid it into his jeans. Together the boys clattered down the stairs and out the back door. They slipped through the hole in the Cyprus hedge that separated their two yards and ran across the grass to the workshop behind the Baily garage.

Inside the shop stood a long workbench under a row of windows. Ron pulled his crystal set out from behind a clutter of tools. "You attach the gismo while I check the aerial."

Carefully Jerry wired the gismo to Ron's crystal radio. He picked the earphones up and slipped them over his head. He could hear the hum of the gismo as he moved the tuner across the coil.

Ron came back. "We should have brought your earphones along, too."

Jerry started to take the headphones off. "I'll go back and get mine," he said.

Ron held his hand up. "No, don't bother. I've got an old telephone in this junk box, somewhere. We can hook that on and listen through the receiver." He bent over and rummaged about in a large box under the workbench. He pushed aside an old world globe, several broken plastic cars, and pulled a dusty old-fashioned standing telephone from the box.

Three wires of different colors, with spade clips on the ends, dangled from the telephone cord. Ron connected a checkered yellow-and-black wire and a brown wire across the capacitor of the crystal radio. The third wire, a checkered black-and-white one, hung free.

Ron jumped up and sat on the workbench. Placing the telephone beside him, he took the receiver from the hook and put it to his ear. The gismo hummed. "A okay," he signaled to Jerry.

There was a crackle of static and the familiar high-pitched voice broke in. "XR...calling XR...we lost your signal for a short while, but it's coming in loud and clear now. Please report back to Base Ship Plymo, if you are able. We repeat: if you are disabled, repair craft are waiting for you at crater 7 del 5, natural satellite, Planet Three, Sun G six zero eight, Syklo Galaxy..."

Jerry glanced at Ron. "Base Ship Plymo...that must be where the message is coming from! I wonder where it is?"

"What I'm wondering is how come this guy is talking in our language. It doesn't figure." Ron scratched his head. "All that the radio astronomers have been able to pull in so far are funny squeaks and blips from outer space. They can't decode them yet, either. This still sounds phony to me!"

"It isn't!" Jerry exclaimed. "Look, Ron, some spaceship named XR is in earth's atmosphere with its communication system knocked out and…" Jerry glanced at the gismo, fading back to pink, and snapped his fingers. *"Hey, wait a minute!"* He pointed at the gismo. "Do you suppose that could be…"

Ron leaned forward. "The communication system to a space-ship?" He shook his head. "It's too little."

"But, Ron, every time we hook the gismo up the little guy says 'we're beginning to receive your transmitting signal loud and clear.'" The high voice cut in "XR…calling XR…we are waiting for your message… XR…calling XR…"

Ron shook his head again. "This is beginning to sound like an endless tape to me!" He was playing idly with the checkered black-and-white wire that hung free from the telephone cord. "XR…" Ron mimicked. "Spaceship XR, where are you?" Grinning, he slipped the spade clip of the black-and-white wire over the free knob of the gismo. He picked the telephone up and held it in front of him like a microphone. He lowered his voice until he sounded like a gruff policeman. "Look, Chief," he said into the telephone mouthpiece, "we're stuck down here on Planet Three in this crazy swamp."

Jerry laughed. He took the phone from Ron's hand and spoke into it. "Yeah, Chief, the sergeant, here, got to watching some majorettes practicing on the football field, and he ran smack into the swamp."

Ron grabbed the phone back from Jerry. "He's wrong, sir, it was the light from their batons that blinded me."

Jerry grinned and leaned over to the mouthpiece. "But don't wor-ry, Chief, nobody's bothered us yet. We're pretending to be swamp gas."

Ron threw his head back and laughed. There was a loud crackle of static. The voice from the radio sounded eager. "Calling XR… We read you! A swamp, did you say? Would you please repeat that message again…slowly…over."

Ron was still chuckling. "Well, Chief, we're…"

Jerry grabbed the phone from Ron's hand. "Cut it, Ron!" His voice was sharp. He slammed the receiver onto the hook.

Ron looked at Jerry. "What did you do that for?"

Jerry's eyes grew rounder as he stared at the phone.

Ron leaned forward. "What's the matter?"

Jerry swallowed and pointed at the phone. "He heard us! That guy *heard* us!"

"So what if he did?"

"Don't you know who that is?"

Ron shrugged his shoulders. "Who else, but some ham operator?"

Jerry's voice was tense. "For gosh sakes, Ron, wise up! That's no ham operator. That man's from *outer space!*"

CHAPTER 4

Park Lane, Planet Three

Planet Three Ron was quiet while Jerry's words sank in. He turned and grinned sheepishly at Jerry. "If he really is a man from outer space, I'll bet our message really shook him, huh?"

Jerry smiled too. "Yeah. Maybe we'd better call him back and tell him it was just a joke."

"You call him, Jerry, I don't know what to say to a spaceman."

"Well, neither do I, except tell him we've found the gismo."

Ron reached over and stroked the furry wires with his fingers. "You really think it's a communication system to a spaceship?"

"There's one way to find out," Jerry said and lifted the receiver on the telephone. "Calling Base Ship Plymo…calling Base Ship Plymo…over." Ron grabbed the earphones and put them over his head.

The static crackled and the high-pitched voice had relief in it. "We read you, XR, go ahead…"

Jerry hesitated. "I'm sorry, sir, about that swamp thing. It was just a joke. This isn't XR calling, this is…its communication system, I guess…what I mean is, I'm Jerry Cole, and I found this gismo, see, and hooked it up to a crystal radio, and that's how I'm talking with you."

"Jerry Cole?" The voice sounded puzzled. "Who are you?"

"Oh, I live here on Earth… Planet Three, that is…you know, near Sun G six zero eight in Syklo Galaxy?"

"An… Earth—ling?" The voice sounded surprised.

"Yes, sir, I guess that's what you'd call me.

There was no sound from the receiver, and Jerry clicked it up and down. "Can you still hear me, sir?"

"Yes, yes... I can hear you... An Earthling, you say. A scientist, no doubt."

"Well, not yet," Jerry said. "I'm in seventh grade...so is my friend here, Ron Baily...he's listening in, too."

"You...you are *children*?"

"Well, not exactly. What is your name, sir?"

There was a long pause as though the listener was thinking and suddenly became aware of the question. "Oh, I'm sorry! My name is Monaal. But why...how..."

Jerry grinned at Ron. "You mean how come I'm talking with you?"

Monaal hesitated again. "Yes...as you say...'how come?'"

"Well, you see I found this gismo in the weeds and..."

"Gismo?"

"Yes, this little rectangular thing. It has knobs on three sides, tiny wires all over the top, and it glows red when you talk."

"Oh that!"

"So I hooked the gismo to my crystal radio set. I heard your message about XR and..."

Ron leaned over to the telephone mouthpiece. "I'm Ron, sir. When I hooked the telephone to the radio, you heard us!"

"Children! Mere children!" Monaal seemed to be talking to himself. "The culture on Planet Three is advancing!"

"Please, Mr. Monaal, could you tell us if this gismo is the communication system for your spacecraft XR?" Jerry asked.

"It's part of the system, yes. Just where did you find it?"

Jerry related his discovery of the gismo.

"Were there power lines close by?" Monaal asked.

"Oh, sure. They run all along the alley," Jerry answered.

"That might explain it." Monaal seemed to be talking to himself again.

"Explain what, sir?" Jerry asked.

"I'm afraid you wouldn't understand, Jerry. That is your name, isn't it?"

"Yes, sir, I'm Jerry."

"Now, Jerry, I'm going to ask you some questions, and I want you to answer them as carefully as you can." Monaal spoke slowly. He sounded like Miss Mills about to give a test.

"Where exactly on Planet Three—Earth, as you call it—are you located?"

Jerry looked at Ron. "Well, sir, that's pretty hard to do unless I'm looking at a map."

"Wait!" Ron jumped down from the workbench. "I've got this old globe here in the junk box. He rummaged under the workbench and brought the dusty globe of the world out. He dusted it clean with his shirttail, and set it on the workbench in front of Jerry.

Jerry turned the globe until the map of the United States faced him. "Mr. Monaal, I have a map now, can you hear me?"

"Yes, Jerry, I read you. Go ahead."

"Well, we're about halfway between the North Pole and the equator in North America—that's the continent with oceans on either side, a big bay at the top, and a big gulf at the bottom…some very large lakes up at the top right-hand corner…"

Monaal's voice broke in, "And a large river running down the center?"

"Yes, the Mississippi River, but it's not quite in the center."

Monaal's voice had a smile in it. "Well, almost in the center. How near to this river are you, Jerry?"

"Not very near. We're about halfway between the Mississippi and the Atlantic ocean…that's the ocean on the right-hand side of the continent."

Ron leaned over. "But we are near a river, sir. We're in a V right between two big ones, the Wabash and the Ohio, in southern Indiana."

Jerry turned. "Look, Ron, he wouldn't know the names of the rivers, and state lines don't show from the air." He turned to the mouthpiece. "We're halfway between the tip of Lake Michigan— that's the big lake farthest down in the continent—and the Gulf of Mexico—that's the gulf at the bottom of the continent."

"Oh, yes! I've found the place where the two rivers come together," Monaal exclaimed.

"Do you have a map, sir?" Jerry asked. "Yes, an exploratory type, but it isn't named like yours." Monaal answered. "Now, Jerry, locate your town for me."

Carefully Jerry described Bridgeville's position between the two rivers. "And Park Lane is where we live. Our houses are right across the street from the park. Ron's is a big white house with a green roof, and mine is the yellow one next door with a white roof."

"Are you in one of those houses right now?" Monaal asked.

"No, we're out in Ron's workshop back of his garage."

"You've done very well in locating yourselves," Monaal said.

Ron leaned over. "Are there really spacecraft flying around our Earth, Mr. Monaal?"

"Why, of course," Monaal said. "Lots of spacecraft!"

"What do they look like?" Ron was eager. "Are they like saucers or cigars or eggs or tops?"

"Saucers? Cigars? I'm afraid I don't know what you're talking about." Monaal sounded puzzled.

"I mean, are the spacecraft round and flat shaped, or long and thin?"

"Well, that depends." Monaal said. "We have many kinds, but the ones from our galaxy that enter Planet Three's atmosphere are usually cylindrical base ships that house the dome-topped explorer discs."

"How big are the explorers?" Jerry asked.

"Oh, many sizes. Some are perhaps eighty feet across, some nearer thirty feet, while some unmanned ones are very small. But you'll have a chance to see one soon, if the description of your location is accurate."

"When?" Jerry and Ron spoke at once.

"When your continent has turned away from your sun and is half-way through the darkness."

"You mean, tonight?" Ron asked.

"Yes, tonight... I must sign off now..."

"Wait, Mr. Monaal, wait! How did you learn our language?" Jerry asked, but it was too late. The voice had clicked off. The gismo was fading back to pink. All that was left was a faint hum.

CHAPTER 5

Spaceship at Midnight

Slowly, Jerry put the telephone receiver back on the hook and began to unwind the wires on the gismo. He grinned at Ron, who was lifting the earphones from his head. "*Now* do you believe me?"

Ron grinned back and laid the headset by the crystal radio. "What do you think! Spaceships tonight! Wow!" He gave the globe a whirl. "'When your continent is halfway through darkness,' that's midnight, right?"

"Right!" Jerry slipped the gismo into his jeans pocket. "Think you can stay awake that long?"

"Are you kidding?" Ron jumped down from the workbench. "I'd stay awake for a week to see a real spaceship!"

"Me, too." Jerry followed Ron out of the shop.

Ron turned. "Hey, tomorrow's Saturday. Bring your sleeping bag over, and we'll camp out here in the yard tonight. That way we can watch for the spaceship together."

"Neat idea!" Jerry exclaimed. "I'll bring my pup tent."

"Okay, but we're sleeping with our heads outside so we can watch the sky. Man! Real spaceships! I can hardly wait. Let's set the tent up right now."

"I'll have to ask Mom." Jerry started for the hole in the hedge.

"Listen, Jerry, don't mention why we want to sleep out. She might not understand. You know how parents are."

"Sure, I know." Jerry smiled back and disappeared through the hedge.

He was back soon, the rolled pup tent balanced on his head. He dropped it on the ground. "Mom says it's okay. Where shall we set the tent up?"

Ron strolled over to a spot near the center of the back lawn. With his hands in his hip pockets, he squinted up at the sky. "How about here? No trees in the way."

Jerry joined Ron and squinted up, too. He lifted his hands, spread them out flat, side by side, circled them around his head, and zoomed them down to flutter in front of him like a hovering saucer. "Okay, spaceship right here, midnight!"

It was growing dusk when they crawled into the pup tent. "I brought along some eats." Jerry pulled an apple from each jean pocket.

"Me, too." Ron held up a box of Whacky Snacks.

Jerry peeled his jeans off and climbed into his sleeping bag. "Mom wanted to know why I was going to bed so early," he said.

Ron grinned. "What did you tell her?"

"I said I was tired."

"Did she buy that?"

"Nope, so I told her you and I had lots of things to discuss."

"Yeah, well, grown-ups don't understand you got to adjust to things a lot when you sleep outside, like this air mattress, for instance. Here, hold my flashlight, Jerry, while I blow this sack up some more."

Jerry held the flashlight and listened to the air wheeze through the air mattress tubes as Ron blew into it. "Wonder what my mom and dad would say if I'd told them we were going to see a real live spaceship tonight."

Ron flipped his thumb over the air mattress valve and screwed the valve shut. "They'd have thought you were kidding."

"Yeah. They'd probably say 'watch out, don't get too close,' like they were going along with a gag."

Ron snaked down into his sleeping bag and pulled the zipper up. "Sure, grown-ups are all alike. They think we're always making things up just to get their attention, or something."

The two boys lay with their heads outside the tent. Crickets chirped in the grass. Far in the distance they could hear the drone of the city street sweeper on its nightly trip around Bridgeville. The stars were beginning to prick through the dark blue above. Jerry put his hands under his head and gazed up at the twinkling lights.

"Where do you suppose he lives? Monaal, I mean," Jerry said.

"Maybe on Mars or Venus," Ron suggested.

"I don't think so."

"Why not?"

"Because if he did, he wouldn't be talking about his galaxy and our galaxy."

"But other galaxies are too far away," Ron said. "Why, it would take a million years for spaceships to come from the nearest galaxy to ours."

"Maybe they don't have the same length years we do. Maybe they've figured out how to live as long as they want to."

Ron rolled over and leaned on his elbow. "But what kind of metal would they use for spaceships that could travel for a million years?"

"Probably some sort of metal we don't even know about. Gases on their planet could be different. Gravity could be different. Everything could be different."

"Yeah," Ron nodded. "Even the people could be different… Two heads, four arms, six feet."

"Not too much different, Ron. They talk like we do. Monaal did anyway."

"That still bugs me," Ron shook his head. "How does he know our language?"

"Maybe they've studied our radio and television signals that are bouncing off our space satellites. If they're advanced enough to build spaceships that travel from one galaxy to another, they're sharp enough to decode our signals."

"But why would they learn to talk our language? What are they up to? Man! I've got a lot of questions to ask Monaal!" Ron reached for the Whacky Snacks box and set it between them.

"Me, too," Jerry sighed and tossed a handful of Whacky Snacks into his mouth.

It was near midnight when Jerry sat up and felt inside his sleeping bag. Ron, heavy-lidded, lay on his back. "What you fussing around for?"

"Oh, a bunch of Whacky Snacks got in here somehow."

"Yeah, I feel a couple in my sack, too, but I'm too tired to look for them. I'm beginning to think Monaal's forgotten all about us. Isn't it about morning?"

Jerry glanced toward the east. "It isn't getting light yet."

Ron rolled over on his side. "I'm going to sleep. Wake me up if anything happens."

"Okay," Jerry threw a Whacky Snack onto the grass and burrowed into his sleeping bag. He turned over and was plumping his pillow when he caught the motion of light toward the north. He sat up. A wedge of tiny stars seemed to be moving across the sky. They grew into globes of light. When they were directly overhead, the leading light glided away from the group and fluttered down like a leaf, growing larger and larger.

Jerry reached over and shook Ron. "Wake up! It's here, Ron, it's here!"

Ron rose sleepily on one elbow. "What's here?"

"The spaceship, stupid! Look!" He pointed at the globe of light which had grown to the size of a large platter. It hovered over the park.

Ron, wide awake now, sat up in his sleeping bag. The glowing disc tilted to one side and glided silently toward the yard. Its brightness faded somewhat, and Jerry could clearly see a wide circle of red and white lights revolving underneath the rim. The spaceship drew nearer and nearer until it blotted out the sky. The crickets had stopped chirping. Jerry was aware of a strange buzzing sound that seemed to come from directly above his forehead. The great spaceship floated over the yard until it reached the garage. There it bobbed not ten feet from the roof with a high, soft whining sound.

Jerry could see the red and white revolving lights reflected on the concave metal surface beneath, where a hatch was sliding open directly in the center. From the brightly lighted interior of the ship, a silver-colored metal wand began to descend slowly.

Jerry and Ron both gasped. On a small platform at the bottom of the wand, stood a little man dressed in a glinting metallic suit.

CHAPTER 6

Anyone home?

Jerry and Ron stared in amazement. The wand from the spaceship touched the roof of the garage, and the spaceman, no taller than Jerry or Ron, stepped onto the ridgepole. He stood for a moment looking down. The red and white lights revolving above him glinted in his round bubble helmet. Their reflection made him seem faceless. A small square box, with a blue light blinking from it, was strapped to his chest. His metallic one-piece suit fitted him like a skin diver's wet suit. His shoes were large and awkward looking. Slowly, the spaceman shuffled to the edge of the roof. Hesitating a moment, he bent his knees and jumped. He floated down to the ground like a maple leaf.

He paused and looked about him, then bent his bubble helmet forward as though he were looking at the box on his chest. He turned slowly. When the blue light blinked directly at the pup tent he stopped moving. Jerry and Ron froze. The spaceman hesitated a moment, then swung around and shuffled toward the workshop. The boys could see him fumble with the knob, push on the door, and go inside.

"What does he want in there?" Ron whispered.

"Don't you remember? That's where we talked to Monaal this afternoon."

"Yeah! I bet he thinks we're still in there," Ron whispered.

"I bet he wants to talk to us some more," Jerry said. He began to climb out of his sleeping bag. "I'm going in there."

"Maybe it isn't safe," Ron whispered. "He might shoot you with a ray gun, or he might be radioactive, or something."

"Are you crazy? He won't hurt me—he knows I'm his friend. Besides, if it's Monaal, I want to ask some more questions."

"Hey, yeah! Me too!" Ron struggled from his sleeping bag. "I'll go with you."

Jerry reached for his jeans. They felt clammy as he stuck his feet into them. He stood up. No time for socks and sneakers. Through the workshop windows, he could see the blue light bobbing about. The spaceman must have climbed onto the workbench, he thought.

Suddenly Jerry felt very awkward. How would he greet the spaceman? What would he say? He was glad Ron would be with him. He glanced down. "Come on, Ron, what's holding you up?"

"These jeans! They're wrong side out."

"Put them on anyway."

Ron snorted. "Ever try to zip a pair wrong side out?" He rose to his knees, and heaved to his feet. "Okay, let's go."

Quickly the boys approached the workshop. The wet grass licked at their bare feet. They had just reached the corner of the building when the blue light blinked at them from the workshop doorway.

"Hi," Jerry's voice sounded very loud in the quiet night.

The spaceman started, then ran clumsily away from the shop.

"Hey, wait! We won't hurt you." Jerry ran after him.

The little man bent forward, touched his boots, and instantly rose into the air. By the time the boys reached the spot where he had been, the spaceman had floated to the garage roof. They could hear his feet patter across the shingles.

Jerry ran backward until he could see the rooftop. "Please, don't go away, please!" He called up.

"We won't hurt you, honest!" Ron chimed in. "Look, we only want to ask you some questions."

By now the spaceman had reached the silver wand. The boys heard him rap sharply on it. Quickly the wand retracted into the ship and carried the spaceman with it. The hatch slid shut. The barely audible whine increased while the red and white lights whirred faster. With a rush of air that swayed the top of the maple tree in Jerry's yard, the spaceship shot upward into the night.

The boys stood in the wet grass and watched the spaceship diminish to a globe of light high above. It joined the waiting wedge of lights that wheeled like a flock of pigeons and streaked northward out of sight.

A window slid up. "Ron?" It was his mother's voice, low and concerned. "Are you two all right?"

"S—sure, we're fine."

"What were you shouting about?"

"Ah, it was nothing, Mom."

"Then please quiet down, or you'll wake the whole neighborhood."

"Okay, Mom."

The boys shuffled toward the tent. Jerry hunched his shoulders and put his hands in his pockets. "Should we tell our folks what happened tonight?"

Ron shook his head. "Not yet. They wouldn't understand."

The boys sat down on their sleeping bags and climbed out of their jeans again. Ron wiped his wet feet with a leg of his jeans. "I still can't figure out why Monaal told us the spaceship was coming and then wouldn't talk with us…just ran away."

Jerry rubbed his feet against the pup tent. "Maybe that wasn't Monaal. Maybe it was some other guy he sent."

"But what did he want in the workshop?"

Jerry inched into his sleeping bag. "I told you—that's where we were when we talked with Monaal this afternoon. Remember?"

Ron pulled up the zipper on his sleeping bag. "But if he thought we'd be in the shop, he must have wanted to see us about something."

"Sure, he probably did."

"Then why did he run away?"

Jerry sank onto his pillow. "I guess I scared him when I ran after him."

Ron put his hands under the back of his head and looked up at the stars. "Man, it's weird! What did that spaceship come all the way down here for?"

The boys were silent. The crickets began to chirp again. Jerry could hear the street sweeper droning down Park Lane. Why had the spaceship come down, he wondered. Suddenly he felt a cold chill run through him. He sat up and reached for his jeans. He felt in the pockets. Thank goodness, it was still there. Slowly he drew the tiny metal object out and held it in his hand. He leaned over. "Ron?"

"Yeah?"

"I bet I know why they came down."

"Why?"

"To get the gismo!"

* * * *

It wasn't until the next afternoon, following Saturday-morning lawn mowing, that Jerry and Ron stepped into the workshop.

"Hey look!" Ron pointed at the workbench. The telephone lay on its side, the stand and mouthpiece removed. The receiver, too, had been taken apart.

Jerry snapped his fingers. "The spaceman! Remember, we could see his blue light blinking through the window like he was doing something on the workbench?"

"Yeah!" Ron fastened the base back onto the telephone and screwed the mouthpiece in place. "Why would he want to wreck it like this?"

"To get at the gismo, stupid! He thought it was inside the telephone."

Ron fastened the telephone to the crystal radio and checked the aerial and ground. He rubbed his hands together. "Okay, let's have the gismo."

Jerry reached into his pockets. He felt first in one pocket, then in the other, but his fingers touched no slippery metal. He looked at Ron in dismay. "It's gone! The gismo is gone!"

CHAPTER 7

Gismo, Gismo, who has the Gismo?

Hastily Jerry felt in his hip pockets, then in his side pockets, but no gismo.

"Maybe it fell into your sleeping bag last night," Ron suggested.

"No, had it this morning. I remember I put it right in here." Jerry slapped his right thigh.

"Got any holes?"

Jerry ran his hands inside his pockets again. "Nope."

"Hey, I know!" Ron exclaimed. "It fell out while you were mowing your lawn."

"Yeah! Let's go look." Jerry ran out of the workshop with Ron after him. The boys dropped to their hands and knees and crawled about on the grass. At last Jerry spied the gismo nearly hidden in a grass clump by the fence. He pounced on it. "Here it is!"

He was brushing the grass clippings from its tiny wires on top when his mother called to him from the back door. "Jerry, may I see you for a minute?"

Jerry shoved the gismo into his pants pocket and scuffed to the steps.

"Here." His mother slipped some money into his shirt pocket. "Run down to Bob's Barber Shop and get yourself a haircut." She reached out and rumpled his red thatch. "You're beginning to look like a troll!"

"Okay, I'll do it later." Jerry turned.

"No, Jerry, not later—now"

"Why not later?"

"Because Bob closes his shop early Saturday afternoons, remember?"

"Aw gee!"

"And please change your jeans. I won't have you running around town with grass-stained knees. Come on, into the house now, chop chop." His mother held the back door open.

Jerry glanced over his shoulder at Ron and sighed heavily. "Guess I'll have to see you later."

Ron ran his fingers through his shaggy hair. "I'll ride down with you. My mom says I need a haircut, too."

Jerry ran up to his room, climbed out of his jeans and into a clean pair. He hurried down the stairs and out the back door. Ron was on his bike cruising back and forth over Dodie's hopscotch. Jerry hopped onto his bike and together they headed for town. They parked their bikes outside the barbershop.

Inside, Jerry and Ron slouched into chairs to wait their turn. Clippers hummed and scissors snipped while they thumbed through the magazines.

Ron jabbed Jerry in the ribs with his elbow. "Hey, look!" He held a picture of a reported UFO sighting. "How about that!"

Jerry took the magazine. "Yeah!" He studied the picture carefully. "That looks just like the one last night. Maybe it's XR."

"Next!" Bob beckoned a pudgy finger at Jerry.

Jerry walked to the barber chair still reading the article.

"What's grabbing you there, son?" Bob asked. He flicked the towel around Jerry's shoulders.

"This article about UFO's." Jerry held the magazine up. "You read it yet?"

Bob clicked his scissors. "Sure, I read all that stuff." He ran a comb through Jerry's hair. "If you ask me, I think it's all a big hoax."

"Don't you believe in ships from outer space?" Jerry winked at Ron.

Bob snipped busily at the top of Jerry's head. "Who does? There's logical explanations for everything we see, son. Maybe those things are lights from airplanes. Maybe they're beacons reflecting on flat clouds. They could even be experimental aircraft from our own country or some other government. From outer space? That's impossible!"

"But if we can figure out spacecraft that fly to the moon," Jerry said, "why can't people from other planets figure out spacecraft that fly from their planet to ours?"

Bob laughed above the hum of clippers. "With little men inside of them, I suppose? You kids and your imaginations!"

Jerry and Ron pedaled home, their heads smelling strongly of cheap cologne. Ron grinned across at Jerry. "I wonder what Bob would have said if we'd told him about last night?"

Jerry shook his head. "No grown-up would ever believe us!"

"Yeah," Ron agreed. "Have I got questions to ask Monaal! Wow! Come on, I'll race you home."

The boys pedaled furiously down Park Lane and up Jerry's driveway. Ron won. Jerry leaned his bike against the maple tree and followed Ron through the hole in the hedge. The two went inside the workshop.

Ron held his hand out. "Okay, the gismo."

Jerry reached into his pockets. "Oh, no! I left it in my other jeans! Be right back." He sprinted out the door and through the hedge, banged into the house, and took the stairs two at a time. He puffed into his room, but no jeans lay by the bed where he had dropped them. He ran to the closet. His mother hadn't hung them up, either. He clattered downstairs again. "Mom," he called loudly, "what happened to the jeans I took off?"

His mother came into the hall with an arm-load of clothes. "They're in the washing machine, why?"

"Oh, no!" Jerry exclaimed. "Did you find the gismo in one of the pockets?"

"The gismo?" his mother asked. "Oh, you mean that little silver brush thing?"

"Yeah, that's it. Where is it?" Jerry asked eagerly.

"I put it on the windowsill on the back porch."

"Thank gosh!" Jerry ran to the back porch, but only a bottle of detergent sat on the windowsill. "It isn't here, Mom!" he wailed.

"Well, someone may have picked it up. Ask Dad, he's in the basement. Ask Lou, or Dodie. They might have seen it."

Jerry hurried down the basement steps two at a time. His father was gluing a rung onto a chair. "Dad, did you by any chance take my gismo off the windowsill on the back porch?"

"Your gismo?"

"Yeah, you know—that metal thing I showed you the other night?"

His father shook his head. "No, I didn't." Jerry rushed up the basement steps, then to the bedrooms upstairs. He leaned panting against Lou's door jam. "You got my gismo, Lou?"

Lou looked up from a magazine. "Your what?"

"My gismo—that metal thing on the windowsill on the back porch."

"You're out of your tree!"

"Have you got it?"

"No!"

Jerry swung around and into Dodie's room, but she wasn't there. He ran downstairs again. "Mom, is Dodie here?"

"I think she's outside somewhere," his mother answered.

Jerry ran to the back door. Dodie was playing hopscotch on the asphalt in front of the garage. He slammed out the back door. "Dodie, did you take anything off the windowsill on the back porch?" he asked.

She turned and looked at him innocently. "What thing?"

"My gismo."

"What would I want with an old gismo, whatever *that* is!" Dodie turned back and carefully threw her lager.

Jerry watched it hit the asphalt with a clink and slide into the last square. Then he gasped in horror. There lay his gismo!

CHAPTER 8

Orders from Monaal

Jerry bent down and scooped the gismo up from the hopscotch square. He shook it in Dodie's face. "Look! *This* is the gismo! And if you've wrecked it, you'll be sorry!" He turned and ran toward the hole in the hedge.

"Mother—r—r!" Dodie wailed, "Jerry has my lager!"

Ron met Jerry in the shop doorway. "What took you so long?"

Jerry wiped his hand across his forehead.

"Man! What I've been through! You wouldn't believe it! But here's the gismo. I hope it's okay."

Quickly he attached it to the crystal radio. Ron slipped the earphones over his head, and Jerry put the telephone receiver to his ear. They listened anxiously for the gismo's hum. It was very faint at first, but gradually grew louder and louder.

Jerry cleared his throat. "This is Jerry Cole calling Base Ship Plymo... Jerry Cole calling Base Ship Plymo..."

There was a sputter of static. "This is Base Ship Plymo, go ahead, please."

"Is this Mr. Monaal?"

"Yes it is, Jerry."

"Sir, we saw the spaceship last night, like you promised we would."

"Yes, I know. You gave us very good directions, Jerry."

"Then it was you who went into the workshop!"

"No, that was one of my men."

"Why did he run away? Didn't you tell him we were his friends?"

"All our men are cautioned not to make contact with inhabitants of other planets, if they are not prepared. He wasn't expecting to see you."

"Then what did he come down for?"

"I think you know the answer to that, Jerry."

"The gismo?"

"Yes."

"But why do you need it back? Couldn't you repair XR with another communication system just like this one?"

"It's a rather important piece of equipment, Jerry. I hope you realize that."

"Oh, yes, sir, I do. But don't you have others you could use? I'd like to keep this gismo, if you don't mind."

"No, Jerry, I'm sorry."

"You mean this is the only one you've got?"

Monaal's voice was earnest. "Can I trust you, Jerry?"

"Sure, Mr. Monaal, sure!"

"Then tonight at midnight bring the gismo to the park."

"Couldn't I keep it just a little while longer, please? If it had fallen in the ocean or on a snowy mountain somewhere, you wouldn't have found it. In fact, you'd never have known where it was at all if Ron and I hadn't hooked it up and told you."

"I know that, Jerry, and I'm grateful to you."

Ron leaned over and spoke into the mouthpiece. "We'd take real good care of it. You see, we've got lots of questions we want to ask you."

"I'm sure you have! I'll see you in the park tonight." Monaal spoke slowly. "Midnight, remember, *with the gismo*. And will you promise me something else?"

"Yes, sir," both boys answered at once.

"Just the two of you."

Jerry sighed. "Yes, sir, just Ron and me. We'll be there. But Mr. Monaal, won't you answer one question now, please?"

Ron leaned over to the mouthpiece quickly. "Yes, sir, please tell us how you learned to speak our language?"

But even as Ron spoke there was a sputter of static, followed by a final click, and the gismo faded from cherry red to faint pink.

Slowly Jerry put the receiver back on the telephone. "He didn't answer us again. Man! I wish I knew why he's got to have the gismo back!"

Ron took the earphones off and laid them on the workbench. "He said it was an important piece of equipment, that's why."

"Sure, I know that! But if they've got lots of spacecraft cruising around this planet, like he said, and they all have communication systems, they must have replacements somewhere." Ron put his chin in his hands. "Maybe the gismos are all back at home base. Maybe they don't have any around here."

"Look, he said repair craft were waiting for XR on the moon, didn't he? Well, they must have some spare parts on the moon."

Ron grinned. "Maybe they're fresh out of gismos up there, too."

"Oh, sure!" Jerry scoffed. "You know something else? He really didn't tell us anything except to meet him tonight and give the gismo back. We'd better sleep outside again tonight."

Ron yawned. "I guess so, but let's take an alarm clock with us and set it for eleven-thirty. I know I won't be able to stay awake that long."

"Okay." Jerry unfastened the gismo from the crystal radio and held it in his hand. "I guess I'd better guard this with my life, huh?"

Ron held his hand out. "Maybe I should hang onto it—you might lose it again."

"Don't worry. I won't lose it. I'm hanging onto this gismo until I see Monaal tonight. And he's not getting it back until he answers a few questions first!"

"That's telling him!" Ron laughed.

That night at supper when Jerry announced he was going to sleep outside, his mother shook her head. "No, Jerry, one night of no sleep is enough."

"I slept last night!" Jerry said indignantly.

"A little, perhaps." His mother smiled. "But those circles under your eyes give you away."

"Please, Mom, I've *got* to sleep outside tonight."

Dodie reached for a slice of bread. "Why?"

"It's none of your business why!" Jerry stabbed at his meat loaf with a fork.

"Jerry," his father said, "watch yourself!" He passed the butter to Dodie. "I'm interested too, Son. Just why must you sleep outside tonight?"

Jerry ducked his head and swallowed a big mouthful of food. "Well, Ron and I…we…just *like* to, that's all. And there's no school tomorrow."

"That doesn't sound like a very urgent reason," his father said. "Your mother's right—you'd better sleep in your own bed tonight. Those circles under your eyes are pretty fierce."

"Oh, Dad!"

"You heard me, Jerry!"

After supper Jerry phoned Ron. "Listen, Ron, I've got a little problem here—my folks. They won't let me sleep outside tonight."

"Yeah? Well, you're not the only one," Ron answered. "Mom says we were too noisy last night. I can't sleep outside either."

"What are we going to do?"

"I guess we'll just have to set our alarm clocks and sneak out at eleven-thirty," Ron suggested.

"Yeah? I guess so, but it's going to be pretty hard here. Dad and Mom usually watch a late movie on TV Saturday nights."

"Maybe you can sneak out the back way between commercials. They won't be wandering around the house then."

"Yeah, I'll try," Jerry said. "Meet you at the hedge at eleven-forty-five, okay?"

"Okay." Ron hung up.

When Jerry went to bed, he set his alarm and put it under the corner of his pillow. If it buzzed too loudly someone would come into his room to see what was up. But it was hard going to sleep with the hum of an electric clock so close to his ear.

Jerry lay thinking about Monaal. What would he look like, he wondered. He would be small like the other spaceman, Jerry felt sure. But what would his face look like? He hadn't been able to see any features of the man the night before. The revolving lights from the spaceship had reflected too brightly on the helmet surface for that. Jerry closed his eyes and let the happenings of the night before slide across his mind. The great floating spaceship…the silver wand…the spaceman…the strange buzzing sound over his forehead…the sound wouldn't stop. It grew louder and louder.

Jerry opened his eyes with a start. The buzzing wasn't over his forehead, it was under his pillow. Quickly he turned the alarm clock off and peered closely at it. Yes, it was eleven-thirty. He swung his feet out of bed. Half an hour and Monaal would be back for the gismo.

CHAPTER 9

The trouble with sisters

Jerry dressed quickly and patted his jeans pocket to make sure the gismo was in there. He pulled on his windbreaker and zipped it up. Quietly he opened his bedroom door. He could hear someone singing loudly on the television in the living room below. The lights in the downstairs hall were out. If he was quiet enough, he could slip through the hall to the kitchen without anyone in the living room hearing him. Jerry was stepping on the top step when he heard the front door bang shut. Lou had just come in from visiting Linda. She called into the living room, then came running upstairs. Jerry backed into his room. As he did so, his heel hit the bottom of the door and it banged against the wall.

Lou switched the upstairs hall light on. "Where do you think you're going?" she asked.

"Sh—h—h!" Jerry held his finger to his lips. "Not so loud. Do you want to wake Dodie up?"

Lou put her hands in the pockets of her slacks. "No, I want to know where you're sneaking off to at this hour, that's all."

"Well it's none of your business, see?" Jerry reached over and snapped off the hall light.

Lou snapped it on again. "Yes, it is my business!"

"Leave me alone, will you?" Jerry reached for the light switch again, but Lou grabbed his arm and twisted it around. Caught off-balance, Jerry went down on his knees. Lou quickly pushed him over onto his stomach and sat down on his back.

The scuffling woke Dodie, and she came out into the hall in her pajamas, rubbing her eyes. "What you fighting for?" she asked sleepily.

"Now see what you've done?" Jerry hissed from the floor. "You woke Dodie up!"

"I woke her up! You're the one that's trying to sneak out!" Lou exclaimed. "Here, Dodie, sit on his legs."

Jerry struggled to push Lou away, but Dodie obligingly plopped herself down on Jerry's legs, and he was pinned to the floor.

Lou folded her arms across her chest. "Okay, Jerry, where were you going?"

"Let me up, you dumb girls!" Jerry fumed.

"Not until you tell us," Lou said.

"Yeah, not till you tell us," Dodie echoed.

"Look, you two, I've got to be in the park in a few minutes. It's very, very important! Now will you quit being funny and get off?"

"Why do you have to be in the park?" Lou asked.

"Yeah, why?" Dodie echoed again.

"I've got to meet somebody, that's why! Let me up, please?"

"Who is it?" Lou insisted.

"Nobody you know!"

"Do I know him?" Dodie asked.

"No!" Jerry struggled to dislodge the girls, but they sat firm. "Okay, I'll tell you. I've got to meet Monaal."

"Who's he?"

"A guy I know."

"Where's he from?"

"You wouldn't believe me if I told you!"

"Go ahead, try me." Lou said.

"Okay, he's from a spaceship."

"That's using your imagination!" Lou grinned.

"No, honest! Probably he's out there waiting for me in the park right now. Go ahead, see for yourself."

"And let you up?" Lou exclaimed. "I'm not that dumb!"

"Don't believe me, then, but the spaceship's there, I know it is!"

Lou turned. "Dodie, you go look out Jerry's window and see if there's a spaceship over the park."

"Okay." Dodie got up and ran into Jerry's room and over to the window.

"It's there, isn't it!" Jerry said.

"No," Dodie answered.

"Ha!" Lou exclaimed. "I knew it was another one of your tricks!"

"There's just a lot of little red and white lights going around in a circle up in the air," Dodie continued.

"That's it!" Jerry exclaimed. "That's the spaceship! Oh, *please* let me up, Lou, *please!"*

The earnestness in Jerry's voice was unmistakable, so Lou stood up. Jerry scrambled to his feet and ran into his room. Lou followed him to the window. The three of them stood looking out at the great spaceship that hovered in the dark sky above the park. The red and white lights rotating slowly under the rim reflected dimly onto the leaves of the treetops below.

"Now do you believe me?" Jerry cried. "I've got to meet Monaal. He's waiting for me over there."

"But why?" Lou asked.

"I'll tell you later. I haven't time now." Jerry started for the door.

"Jerry, wait!" There was concern in Lou's voice. "Is it safe to go out there?"

"Sure it's safe. Last night the spaceship went right over us. That's why I wanted to sleep outside again tonight." Jerry stopped at the doorway. "Listen, don't tell anyone about this spaceship, promise, Lou?"

"Okay."

"Promise, Dodie?"

"I promise."

Jerry reached out to turn the hall light out when his father called up the stairs. "Is everything all right up there, Lou?"

Jerry beckoned frantically to his sister.

Lou hurried to the door and stuck her head out. "Everything's okay, Daddy."

Dodie came padding toward the door. "Hey, Daddy, guess what? There's a spa—" she began, but Jerry cupped his hand over her mouth and held her struggling against him.

"Sh—h—h!" he hissed into her ear. "You promised not to tell!"

"Do I hear Dodie? Is she still awake up there?" Mr. Cole called.

"Oh, no," Lou said hastily. "She's just talking in her sleep."

"Well, turn the light out, Lou, and try to be a little quieter or you will wake her up. Good night."

"Good night, Daddy." Lou reached over and turned out the hall light.

"Thanks, pal," Jerry whispered. He released Dodie and peered down the stairs, then drew back. "Darn! He's in the kitchen now. I can't get out."

"Why don't you go through your window and down the maple tree?" Lou suggested.

"Yeah, I guess I'll have to." Jerry ran to the window and raised it softly. He unhooked the screen and straddled the window ledge. The gentle slope of the front porch roof was only a few feet below. Quietly he eased himself out onto the shingles and crept toward the maple tree branch that curved over the porch. He climbed onto it and shinnied toward the trunk. Lou and Dodie stood with their heads out the window watching him. He lowered himself from branch to branch and jumped lightly to the ground.

He turned to run toward the park. In the gloom, he didn't see his bike. Down he went in a clatter of foot pedals and handlebar, his right foot turning under him. Sharp pain stabbed through his ankle.

Soon the front door squeaked open, and he could hear his father's footsteps on the front porch coming toward him. Quickly Jerry crawled behind the tree and held his breath. His father peered over the porch railing at the bike lying on the grass, then turned.

"It was just Jerry's bike that fell over, Alice," his father said. "That boy has got to learn to put his things away!" The front door squeaked shut again.

Jerry looked toward the hole in the hedge. Ron wasn't there. Was he over in the park, or had he overslept, Jerry wondered. It didn't matter. What mattered now was getting the gismo to the park.

Jerry pulled himself up and tried to step on his right foot, but it wouldn't hold him and he fell again. He looked toward the park. He had promised Monaal he'd be there at twelve. How could he keep his promise?

CHAPTER 10

To the park by sister power

Jerry sat on the ground at the foot of the maple tree and leaned forward. He closed his eyes and rubbed his ankle. Tears of pain and anger squeezed out from under his eyelids. How could he have been so clumsy! He couldn't go to the park by himself.

He couldn't climb back up the tree. If he went in the house by the front or back door, he'd have to hop on one foot, and his parents would be sure to hear him. There would be all kinds of explaining to do. And they probably wouldn't believe a thing he told them about the gismo, the spaceship, and Monaal. He was really in a mess now!

"*Psst*, Jerry!" It was Lou. She was peering down at him from the edge of the porch roof. "What happened?" she whispered.

"I ran into my dumb bike and turned my ankle!" Jerry whispered back. "I can't stand on it. Lou, you've got to help me!"

"Okay, but how?"

Jerry thought a minute. "If I could hang onto someone I think I could make it over to the park."

"Hi!" Dodie's round face appeared beside Lou.

Lou turned. "Go back, Dodie!" she whispered. "You're in your pajamas! It's too cold out here for you."

"No it's not. I've got my bathrobe on, see?" Dodie stood up to show Lou.

Her older sister pulled her down quickly. "Don't stand on the edge of the roof like that! You'll fall off!"

"What's Jerry sitting there for?" Dodie whispered.

"He's hurt his ankle," Lou said. "Now keep quiet or they'll hear us downstairs." Lou looked over the edge of the roof. "Listen, Jerry," she whispered, "I'll come down, and you can hang onto me."

"How're you going to get down here?"

"The same way you did. I haven't forgotten how to climb down a tree."

"Okay, but be real quiet," Jerry warned. Lou slung her leg over the branch and inched along till she reached the tree trunk. Slowly she lowered herself branch by branch till she could jump to the ground.

"I'm coming, too." Dodie was halfway down the maple before Jerry noticed her.

"Oh, Dodie, go back!" Jerry whispered in exasperation.

Dodie dangled by her arms from the lowest branch, her feet still a long way from the ground. "Catch me, Lou."

"I thought I told you to go back!" Lou reached up and helped her sister to the ground.

"I want to help, too," Dodie whimpered.

"Well, just keep quiet, then," Jerry pleaded.

Lou extended her hand toward him. "Here, Jerry, grab hold." Jerry heaved himself to his good foot. Lou put her arm around him, and he put his arm over her shoulder. "Now, can you hop okay?" Lou asked.

Jerry hopped a step. "Yeah, I can make it."

Dodie walked around to his other side and put her arm around him. "You can lean on me, too," she whispered.

Jerry put his hand on Dodie's shoulder and, with a sister on either side, hopped down the driveway and across the street.

Their footsteps echoed through the empty park. Crickets chirped in the grass. Off in the distance Jerry could hear the drone of the street sweeper coming down Park Street. Jerry looked up. Through the treetops he could see the red and white lights of the spaceship wink on and off, as it circled slowly above the park.

"Where are you supposed to meet this spaceman?" Lou asked.

"He didn't say where…just come to the park," Jerry answered.

"How did you talk to him?" Lou asked.

"Remember that gismo I found?"

"That thing that looks like a mouse?" Lou exclaimed.

"My hopscotch lager?" Dodie asked.

"Stupid girls!" Jerry muttered.

Lou drew her arm away. "Okay, Jerry Cole, if we're so stupid, you can go the rest of the way alone. We just asked a couple of simple questions. Come on, Dodie."

Jerry grabbed Lou's arm. "Don't go! I'm sorry, I didn't mean that—it just slipped out. The gismo…it's a communication system from a spaceship."

Lou took hold of him again. "How did you find out?"

"I hooked it up to my crystal radio and Ron hooked on his telephone and we got this guy, Monaal. He told us what the gismo was and said he wanted it back. We saw the spaceship last night, but the spaceman Monaal sent down got scared, or something, and we didn't get to talk to him. Monaal's coming tonight, and, man! Have I got questions to ask him!"

They had reached the center of the park where a bandstand filled the clearing, its roof, a soft round shadow against the night sky. Jerry looked up. "Here it comes!" He pointed at the circling lights that slowly floated into view over the clearing.

The spaceship dipped slightly, and the lights reflected along its curved metal surface. Slowly it came to a stop directly above the bandstand roof. The hatch underneath slid open and the silver-colored wand began to descend with a little man in a metallic-colored suit clinging to it. He stepped to the roof, slid to the edge, gave a jump, and floated to the ground. As before, his bubble helmet reflected the lights above, and Jerry couldn't see his face. The spaceman turned slowly until his blinking blue light shone in the direction of the children.

"Come on, let's go," Jerry said and tried to hop forward. But his two sisters stood rooted to the ground, their eyes wide with astonishment.

Jerry tugged forward impatiently. "Don't be scared, that's just Monaal. He won't hurt us."

Hesitantly, the girls moved forward with Jerry supported between them.

A strange urgent beeping sound suddenly came from the space-ship. As the children neared the spaceman, he began to back away.

"It's only me, Monaal," Jerry reassured. But the spaceman bent forward and with a leap, floated to the bandstand roof.

"Monaal, please don't be frightened. I'm Jerry, remember? You talked with me…and I've brought the gismo, like you asked me to."

Monaal's answer was a sharp tap on the wand of the spaceship. He rode upward, the hatch slid closed, and with a high whine, the spaceship tilted to one side and rose rapidly toward the stars.

"Now why did he run away this time!" Jerry exclaimed.

"Maybe we frightened him," Lou said.

"Yeah," Dodie said. "Maybe he thought we had three heads and six feet."

"Oh, Dodie!" Jerry sighed. "We'd better go home. He won't be back again tonight."

"Are you sure?" Lou asked.

"Well, he didn't come back again last night."

The girls swung around, and Jerry hopped between them down the echoing sidewalk toward Park Street. They were nearly there when they saw the white form of a large street sweeper parked beside the curb. They could hear voices coming toward them.

Quickly, Lou pulled Jerry and Dodie behind the dark branches of a holly bush beside the walk.

Two men in coveralls clicked by. "So the street sweeper stalled! That's not so unusual, Charlie."

"But I tell you it was that…that *thing* up there did it when it flew over us." The second voice sounded shaken.

"Looked like it stopped about over the bandstand, didn't it?"

"Yeah, right about here." The two men paused in the clearing.

"Well, it isn't here now, that's for sure!"

The children could hear the voices coming back.

"This is the second night that thing's been around, Bill."

"Yeah, I know. Look, Charlie, we'd better keep quiet about this. Folks would never believe us if we said we'd seen a flying saucer."

"You're right, Bill, they'd never believe us!" The two men walked by. The children heard the sweeper start and drone on down the street. As soon as it was out of sight, they hurried as fast as Jerry could hop across the street and up the driveway of their house. The lights were still on in the living room.

"Good!" Jerry whispered. "Dad and Mom are downstairs."

"But how are we going to get back inside?" Lou asked.

"Let's just walk in the front door," Dodie suggested.

"Are you crazy?" Jerry exclaimed. "They'd ask us all sorts of questions and find out about the spaceship. Remember, this is a secret just between us kids, and you're *not* to tell anyone. Promise, Dodie?"

"Okay, I promise," Dodie said.

But Jerry felt uneasy, somehow. Dodie's promises weren't too reliable. He would have to watch her.

CHAPTER 11

Keeping Dodie quiet

The three stood under the maple tree in the dim light of the midnight stars. Jerry balanced on his good foot and leaned against the trunk. "I guess we'll have to get back in the house the same way we came out. Think you can reach that lower limb by yourself, Lou?"

"Sure, no problem," Lou whispered back.

"Then you and Dodie give me a lift to the first branch. If I don't have to jump, I can make it from there."

"I can't jump that high, either," Dodie said.

"Lou'll help you after I climb up," Jerry said. "Now everyone be real quiet! Lou, you and Dodie put your hands together and make a step," he ordered. Jerry leaned heavily on the girls' shoulders and hopped his good foot into their waiting hands. They lifted him up a short distance. He grabbed for the branch and swung himself onto it. He worked his way slowly up the tree to the branch overhanging the porch. He straddled this limb and inched along toward the roof, where he eased himself carefully onto the shingles.

He turned. "Okay, Lou," he whispered down, "lift Dodie up. I'll help her onto the roof."

Lou picked Dodie up around the middle, and she began to giggle. "Oh, be quiet, Dodie!" Jerry hissed down at her. Dodie tried hard to stop as she climbed up the maple branches, but on reaching Jerry she broke into a fresh burst of giggles.

Jerry cupped his hands roughly over her mouth. "Will you shut up?" he whispered fiercely. "If Mom and Dad hear us, we've had it! Now get back into the room!" Dodie turned and crept across the porch roof to Jerry's window. "Okay, Lou, come on up." Jerry beckoned to his older sister.

Lou jumped, caught the limb, and swung herself into the tree. In a few moments, she was safely on the roof beside Jerry. Together they turned and crawled back to the bedroom window. Lou helped Jerry in, climbed in herself, and hooked the screen.

Jerry sank to the floor. "We made it! Oh, man, what a night!"

Lou sat down beside him. "You said it. If I live to be a hundred, I'll never forget that spaceship and that weird little man."

Dodie plopped down on the rug between them. "Me neither!"

"Well, don't ever tell, Dodie," Jerry cautioned.

"I won't, I won't."

"Look," Jerry said, "be a good kid and go back to bed."

"Yes, hurry!" Lou said, "Mom and Dad have turned the television off."

Dodie jumped up and scampered across the hall.

While Jerry rolled onto his hands and knees and headed for his bed, Lou tiptoed to the door. She turned. "I'm sorry about sitting on you, Jerry, I didn't know…

"That's okay," Jerry heaved himself onto the bed.

"What are you going to do now? About the gismo, I mean?" Lou asked.

"I haven't figured out yet." Jerry put his head on his pillow. "You won't tell anybody about tonight, will you?"

"Are you kidding?" Lou exclaimed. "Nobody would believe me if I did. Oh, oh! Here they come. Gotta go."

Jerry raised his head. "Thanks for helping, Lou," he whispered.

* * * *

The next morning Jerry hobbled downstairs to breakfast, late. He hadn't been able to lace his sneaker over the swollen ankle.

Mrs. Cole broke an egg into the skillet. "What's the matter with everyone this morning? Your eyes all look like burned holes in a blanket! Didn't any of you get enough sleep?"

Mr. Cole reached for the toast. "Morning, Jerry, what happened to your foot?"

Jerry sat down at the table. "Oh, nothing much, just turned it a little."

"Yeah!" Dodie took a big bite of toast. "He fell over his…"

"Dodie!" Jerry said loudly, glaring across the table at her.

His father looked up sharply at him.

Jerry caught his father's look. "Dodie," he growled, "You've got jam on your face."

"I know its early, Jerry," his father said, "but there's no need to talk roughly to your sister. By the way, young man, you forgot to put your bike away last night."

"Yeah, I *know*… I mean, I know."

"If you want your things to last, Jerry, you'd better get into the habit of taking care of them. Your bike goes in the garage."

"Yes, sir." Jerry glanced sideways at Lou, who hid a smile behind a sip of cocoa.

His mother came to the table. "Let me see that foot, Jerry."

"It's okay, Mom, really it is."

She knelt beside his chair. "Let me see it." He held his foot out.

His mother turned the pants leg up. "Why, you can't even tie your shoelace around that ankle! It's back to bed for you!"

"Oh, Mom!"

His mother eased his shoe off. "How on earth did you do a thing like that!"

Jerry glared across at Dodie. "I fell over…something, that's all." Lou joined in the glaring, and Dodie ducked her head.

"We'll soak that ankle after breakfast, then get your weight off of it," his mother said. "You look like you could use a little rest anyway."

Jerry was glad his mother didn't ask him any more questions while she helped him upstairs, soaked his ankle, and tucked him back into bed. He hoped Lou would be able to keep Dodie quiet about what had happened the night before.

That afternoon Ron came up to visit Jerry. "Your mom says you hurt your ankle. What happened?"

"Where were *you* last night, Ron? Man, could we have used you!"

"It was that stupid alarm clock...didn't go off. Guess it wasn't set right or something."

"I figured as much!" Jerry nodded.

"But what happened to your ankle?" Ron asked. "Did you see Monaal?"

Jerry told him of the night's adventures. "I'd sure like to know why Monaal backed off that way," he finished.

"Yeah, it's weird!" Ron said.

Jerry sat up in bed. "Listen, go get your telephone and earphones, and we'll hook the gismo up right here!" He slapped his night-stand.

When Ron returned, they fastened the gismo carefully to the radio set and attached the earphones and telephone.

"Better close the door, Ron," Jerry said.

Ron was latching the door when Dodie pushed against it. Ron looked at Jerry. "You want your kid sister in here?" he asked.

"Heck, no!" Jerry said.

"Sorry, Dodie, you've got to stay out." Ron braced his foot against the door.

"You better let me in or I'll tell about last night!" Dodie yelled through the door.

"Brat!" Jerry exclaimed. "Okay, let her in."

Dodie bounced into the room. "I didn't tell anybody, Jerry. I wanted to, but I didn't tell."

"Good girl. Now sit down and be quiet. We've got to hear something." Jerry took the receiver off the hook.

There was a light knock on the door, and Lou stuck her head in the room. "Okay if I come in?"

"Sure," Jerry said, "Might as well, everyone else is in here."

Lou walked over and gazed down at the crystal set with the maze of wires attached to it. "Is that the gismo?" She pointed at the tiny wires glowing pink now.

Jerry nodded and signaled for quiet. "I'm trying to get Monaal. "This is Jerry Cole calling Base Ship Plymo... Jerry Cole calling Base Ship Plymo...come in, please."

Ron slid the earphones over his head.

"I want to listen, too," Dodie said.

Jerry motioned for her to be quiet.

"If you don't let me listen, I'll—"

Jerry rolled his eyes. "Go ahead, Ron, hook up my earphones and turn 'em so Dodie and Lou can listen."

Ron fastened Jerry's headset onto the crystal radio and turned the earphones out. Lou sat down beside Dodie, and they put their ears to the set.

"This is Jerry Cole calling Base Ship Plymo… Come in, please." Jerry repeated.

Sudden static crackled. "This is Base Ship Plymo, go ahead."

"Monaal?"

"Yes, Jerry?"

"Why did you back away from us last night?"

"There were three of you, Jerry. Who were the others?"

"Oh, those were my sisters, Lou and Dodie."

"I thought we agreed no one but you and Ron were to meet me?"

"We did, sir, but I turned my ankle and couldn't walk, and Ron's alarm clock didn't work so he overslept, and I had to get my sisters to help me come to the park. Was it because of my sisters that you left?"

"No, Jerry, we detected a vehicle approaching."

"That must have been the street sweeper," Jerry exclaimed. "Did you stall their machine?"

"Only temporarily."

"Man, were they shook!" Jerry laughed. "They came looking for you after you left."

"We were afraid they would. Now listen closely, Jerry. Since it will take a little time for your injury to mend, we will delay our next trip. Take good care of yourself and the gismo, but don't try to contact us. We will be elsewhere in your galaxy. When your planet has turned six rotations, however, we will return."

"That's in six days, isn't it?" Jerry asked.

"Yes," Monaal answered, "halfway through darkness."

"Where will we meet you?"

"To make it easier, we will descend over your house and meet you outside. I hope your ankle will be better by then."

"Thanks, Mr. Monaal, it will be."

"And this next time, Jerry," Monaal spoke slowly, *"nothing* must go wrong...*nothing!"* There was a flurry of static.

"Mr. Monaal, sir?" Jerry said, but there was no answer. The gismo had faded back to silver.

CHAPTER 12

Seven hundred years old?

Jerry put the receiver back on the hook and ran his fingers through his hair. "Darn! I'll never find out where Monaal comes from or how his spaceship gets here if he hangs up on me all the time!"

Ron took his headphones off. "Yeah, or how he learned our language."

Lou laid the headphones she shared with Dodie in her lap. "Maybe he doesn't want you to know."

Jerry shook his head. "It sure looks that way."

Dodie wandered over and picked the telephone up. She lifted the receiver off the hook. "Calling Base Ship Plymo... Base Ship Plymo...come in, please," she mimicked Jerry.

Jerry grasped at the phone. "Dodie! Don't fool around with that!"

Dodie moved out of his reach. "I just want to ask Monaal something."

Jerry leaned out of bed. "Well he isn't there anymore. Give me the phone!"

Dodie stretched the distance of the wires just beyond Jerry's reach. "Hi! Are you Mr. Monaal?" Dodie spoke into the phone. "I'm Dodie... Yes... Jerry's sister... I saw you the other night in the park, remember?"

"Hey!" Ron picked his earphones up. "She's talking with him!"

Jerry nearly fell out of bed. "Dodie, give it here!" Then he turned to Lou. "Quick, hand me that other headset!" Lou held the earphones so Jerry could listen, too.

Monaal was speaking again. "You were helping your brother?"

"Yes," Dodie nodded. "Mr. Monaal, you're so little. How old are you?"

"Dodie!" Jerry exclaimed, "That's not..."

"I'm seven hundred years old by our calendar."

"Seven hundred years old!" Dodie exclaimed. "Why are you so small, then?"

"The planet Throal, where I live, is beyond your galaxy. It is very old and very large, much larger than your planet, and many people live on it. We have grown smaller so that there will be enough space and food for everyone who wants to stay there."

"You mean you shrink everyone down to your size?"

"No, Dodie, over hundreds of years we have developed smaller bodies."

"Do you have families like ours?"

"Yes, we do."

"Do you have a little girl like me?"

"Yes, her name is Kaali."

"Oh, I like Kaali! How big is she?"

"Well," chuckled Monaal, "she's not as big as you are."

"Is she half as big as you are, Mr. Monaal?"

"Just about…maybe a bit smaller."

Dodie held her hand out to the height she remembered Monaal, then lowered her hand halfway. "Why then she'd be only two feet high! Oh, I'd like to see Kaali! Does she play hopscotch?"

"Dodie!" Jerry exclaimed. "Don't bother him with stupid questions like that! Ask him what makes his spaceships fly."

Dodie looked at Jerry. "You ask him your questions and I'll ask him mine!"

"Then give me the phone!" Jerry made another grab for it.

"No!" Dodie turned away from him. She spoke into the mouthpiece. "Does Kaali play bounce ball against your garage door?"

Monaal's voice had a smile in it. "She plays lots of games, but I'm not familiar with their names. I haven't been home for some time, but I will be seeing her soon."

"Then ask her if she likes to play hopscotch and bounce ball, will you, please?"

"I will."

"Good-bye."

"Good-bye, Dodie."

Dodie put the receiver on the hook and set the phone on Jerry's nightstand. "I like Mr. Monaal. He's a nice man."

Jerry laid the headset down and grabbed the telephone. "Mr. Monaal?" He clicked the receiver up and down, but no one answered.

He put the phone back and thumped his covers with his fists. "Why couldn't he answer me! Of all the dumb questions to ask him, Dodie! Hopscotch! Bounce ball! Why couldn't you ask him important things? Now we'll never learn anything from him!"

Lou stood up. "We learned where he comes from—the planet Throal in another galaxy—and why he's so little."

"Sure," Dodie agreed. "And he's got a family and a little girl named Kaali."

"Yeah," Ron added. "And he's seven hundred years old! Wow!"

"What's so important about that!" Jerry fumed.

Lou walked toward the door. "Well, for one thing, it proves that we're not the only planet in the universe with people on it."

"Sure," Ron said, "and if they can all live to be seven hundred years old, they must have figured out a lot of things, like how to get rid of diseases and accidents and war."

"Yes, but their spaceships," Jerry said. "What are they made out of? How do they fly? Why are they flying around the Earth? *That's* what I want to know. And thanks to Dodie, I won't find out till I see Monaal next Saturday midnight!"

"Why are you mad at me?" Dodie asked. "You wouldn't give me back the phone when Monaal was talking, that's why!"

"He was talking to me!"

"He was talking to me before that!"

"Well, you were through!"

"I was not! The static came, he didn't answer, so I thought... Oh, skip it! Go on out and play hopscotch!" Jerry plunked back on his pillow and stared at the ceiling.

* * * *

The six days of waiting was a long time for Jerry. He tucked the gismo far back in his underwear drawer, and took it out each morning when he dressed. Whenever he held it in his hand, he thought of another question he wanted to ask Monaal. His ankle improved rapidly, and soon he was pedaling to and from school.

Friday afternoon Jerry coasted up the driveway with Ron just behind him. With his bike parked in the garage, Jerry shuffled beside

Ron who was wheeling his own bike toward the hole in the hedge. Jerry stuffed his hands in his pockets. "Well, tomorrow night is UFO night!"

"Yeah!" Ron exclaimed. "Only it should be IFO—Identified flying object."

Jerry grinned. "I bet we're the only ones around here who can say that."

"Sure we are!" Ron agreed. "And when we get through asking Monaal a bunch of questions tomorrow night, we'll be smarter than the space program guys!"

"Yeah, maybe." Jerry stopped at the hedge. "Look, how are you going to wake up, Ron, if your alarm clock doesn't work?"

"Oh, it works okay," Ron answered. "When I set it last time, I forgot to pull out the knob on the back. Don't worry, I won't miss being over here this time!"

* * * *

Saturday night, when his alarm went off under his pillow, Jerry was out of bed and into his clothes in a matter of seconds. He opened his chest of drawers softly, and pulling the gismo out, dropped it into his pocket. He stuffed his arms into his jacket and zipped it up. Quickly he crossed to the door and stood in the hall listening to the mutter of the Saturday night movie on the television. It was obviously the middle of a scene. If he was fast, he could make it downstairs and through the kitchen before the commercial.

Jerry tiptoed softly down the steps and through the hallway. He crossed the kitchen and was almost to the back porch when the kitchen light snapped on.

"Jerry! Just a minute. Where are you going?" It was his father!

CHAPTER 13

But I promised Monaal—

Jerry blinked in the sudden brightness of the kitchen light. Why couldn't he have been a little quicker, he thought. He forced a smile.

"Hi, Dad, I'm just going outside for a few minutes. Be right back." He turned toward the back porch.

"Do you know what time it is, Jerry?" His father pointed at the kitchen clock. "Look!"

"Sure, I know…almost midnight. I've got to meet someone then."

"Who?" his father asked.

"Nobody you know, Dad."

"I don't like this, Jerry."

"It's okay, honest. I've got to give this gismo back." Jerry took the gismo from his pocket.

"Oh, then you found out who it belongs to?"

"Sure."

"By the way, just what is it?"

"A communication system."

"To what?"

Jerry dropped his eyes. "I can't tell you. You wouldn't believe me."

"What makes you think I wouldn't?"

Jerry looked up. "Because…well, because grown-ups think there's a logical explanation for everything."

"Isn't there?"

"Not for this gismo!" Jerry cupped it in his hand. "Look, Dad, I've got to go outside!"

"Just a minute, Son!" His father came towards him. "What's so mysterious about the gismo?"

"Well, it's…it's from a spaceship!"

"How do you know?"

"That's a long story, Dad, I'll tell you later. Right now I've got to give this gismo back."

"Back to who?"

"Monaal, the spaceman."

"Spaceman! Now see here, Jerry, this has gone far enough! Just why do you want to go outside at midnight? Tell me the truth!"

"I have, Dad!" Jerry protested. "I've got to give this gismo back to Monaal. It's a communication system that fell off of some spacecraft named XR. Monaal's out there waiting for me right now!"

"You think I'll believe this?" His father's voice was beginning to sound angry.

"Dad, honest, I'm telling the truth! Come outside and see for yourself! The spaceship should be hovering over the house right now." Jerry ran for the back door and his father strode after him.

Even as he ran down the back steps, Jerry could hear the strange buzzing like a swarm of bees directly over his forehead. He backed away from the house and looked up. The soft whine of the motor floated down, but tonight no circling red and white lights glinted on the convex bottom. Only the great circle of the spaceship, like an enormous black shadow as large as the house, blotted out the stars.

"See, Dad, there it is!" Jerry pointed to the bobbing shape.

Ron came running from the hole in the hedge. "They just came down, Jerry." Then Ron saw Mr. Cole, and whispered into Jerry's ear, "Hey, how come your dad's here?"

"I couldn't get out of the house without him," Jerry whispered back.

Mr. Cole stood rooted to the ground. His mouth gaped open at the great dark spaceship floating over the house. Suddenly he seized both boys by their arms. His voice was urgent. "Into the house, both of you."

"But Dad! I promised Monaal…"

Mr. Cole paid no attention to Jerry's protest, but hurried the boys up the back steps and into the house. He walked them through the hallway and into the living room where Mrs. Cole was trying vainly to clear the heavy snow on the television set. He plunked the two boys onto the couch. "Turn the television off, Alice, I want you to hear this." He pulled a chair up and sat facing the boys, and held his hand out. "Jerry, let me have that gismo." His voice shook a little as he spoke.

Jerry handed the gismo to his father.

"Now," his father commanded, "I want you to tell me everything you've found out about the gismo—everything, do you hear?" The boys looked at each other. The authority in Mr. Cole's voice was unshakeable. They couldn't keep the secret of the gismo any longer. Their words tumbled over one another as Jerry and Ron told of their experiments with the gismo…of their conversations with Monaal… of their two meetings with the spacemen. Mr. and Mrs. Cole listened intently.

"And now, Dad," Jerry finished, "please give me the gismo so I can return it to Monaal. I promised him I would."

Mr. Cole looked at the gismo, then at Jerry. "Do you know how important this piece of metal is, Jerry?"

"Of course I do!" Jerry replied.

His father looked earnestly into Jerry's face. "This gismo can unlock the secrets of the universe that have been puzzling our scientists for ages!"

"I know, Dad, but I promised Monaal, and we've got questions to ask him."

"This should be in the hands of our space engineers. *They* are the ones who should be asking the questions, not a couple of boys!" Mr. Cole said and looked at his watch. "If we leave now we can be at the U.S. Air Force base by morning." He turned to Mrs. Cole. "I'm taking the boys with me. The authorities will probably want to question them."

"Mr. Cole," Ron said, "Lou and Dodie saw the spaceship, and Dodie talked with Monaal, too."

"Then they must go along with us. Alice, wake the girls and get them ready. Dodie can rest in Jerry's sleeping bag in back of the station wagon."

It was nearly one o'clock in the morning when Mr. Cole herded everyone onto the front porch. The girls giggled and shivered as Mr. Cole made them wait while he peered cautiously up. But the spaceship was gone, and he beckoned for everyone to hurry to the garage.

Mr. Cole backed the car out and headed down Park Street. Jerry sat beside his father and watched the headlights tunnel into the night. "Dad?"

"Yes, Jerry?"

"Could I please hold the gismo...just till we get there?"

"Yes, I guess so. It's in my coat pocket next to you."

Jerry reached in his father's pocket and drew the gismo out. He held it in one hand and stroked the fur-like wires on top. Where was the spaceship now, he wondered. What did Monaal think of him, especially when he had said "nothing must go wrong, this time, nothing," and everything had! His father was right about the gismo unlocking the secrets of the universe, but was it fair to use it this way after Jerry had promised to give it back? To break a promise to someone—even someone from another planet—wasn't right. He wished he had never found the gismo!

It was quiet as they drove through the long night. Lou and Ron dozed in the back seat. Dodie bounced about adjusting the sleeping bag in the rear of the station wagon. Mr. Cole seemed lost in thought, and Jerry was too miserable to say anything. He sat staring at the gismo.

The highway they followed, deserted now in the early hours before dawn, lay across long stretches of cornfields and low, rolling pasture land. They had come to a rise in the road, when the car motor died suddenly, the lights went out, and the station wagon rolled to a stop.

Jerry leaned forward. "What's wrong, Dad?"

His father tried to start the car, but nothing happened. "I don't know Jerry, the electrical system is out, I guess."

A familiar buzzing sound directly over Jerry's forehead made him sit up. He looked at his father with wide eyes. "I know why it stalled," he said in a low voice.

"Why?" his father asked.

"The spaceship is over us!"

CHAPTER 14

The new Gismo

Straining against his seat belt, Jerry leaned forward and peered out of the windshield. He pointed up. "Look, Dad!"

His father leaned forward, too, then drew his breath in. Circling red and white lights floated above them reflecting on the car hood. The spaceship drew ahead of them and hovered above the asphalt road. At the bottom of the ship, the hatch slid open and the silver wand descended slowly. A dozen little men clung to it, the blue lights on their chests blinking. When the wand touched the road, the men jumped off and, spreading out into a half circle, walked toward the car.

Lou, Ron, and Dodie awakened by the sudden stop, stared wide-eyed at the approaching spacemen.

One figure separated from the others and stepped forward.

"It's Monaal!" Jerry exclaimed. "He's come for the gismo!" Jerry turned to his father. "Dad, I know you have a point about keeping the gismo, but I've *got* to give it back." He unfastened his seat belt, slid across the seat, and opened the car door.

"I'll go with you, Jerry." His father followed him, while Ron, Lou, and Dodie piled out of the back seat. They stood by the side of the road, a circle of blinking blue fights surrounding them.

Monaal lifted the front of his space helmet. In the dim fight of the sky just before dawn, Jerry looked into a kind and smiling face of a handsome little man. His voice was high-pitched and friendly. "I hope we didn't frighten you too much, but it was most necessary we contact you."

"That's okay, Mr. Monaal," Jerry said. "I'm sorry I couldn't meet you back at my house, but, ah…things came up I hadn't figured on."

Monaal nodded. "I thought so."

"This is my father, Mr. Cole," Jerry said.

The spaceman bowed ever so slightly. "It's a pleasure to meet the father of such an intelligent boy."

Mr. Cole reached down and shook Monaal's hand. "Thank you, sir."

"And this is Ron and Lou and Dodie." Jerry motioned to each in turn. Monaal greeted each one with a bow.

Dodie squeezed between Jerry and Mr. Cole. "Hi, Mr. Monaal. I'm Dodie, remember?"

Monaal smiled warmly at her. "Yes, indeed, I remember you. I saw my own little girl, Kaali, over our intergalactic communication screen, and I told her about you."

"Did you ask her about hopscotch and bounce ball?"

"Yes, but she calls them by different names."

"Oh, I wish I could play hopscotch with Kaali! We could have lots of fun together."

"I'm sure you could," Monaal smiled and turned to Jerry. "I think you know why we're here."

Jerry nodded. "Yes, sir, you came for the gismo."

Monaal looked up at Mr. Cole. "I'm sure you'll agree with me that the gismo is *not* a child's toy."

Mr. Cole nodded vigorously. "I certainly do!"

Jerry held the gismo tightly in his fist. "Before I give the gismo back, sir, would you please answer a few questions for me?"

"If I can, Jerry," Monaal said.

"What makes your spacecraft go?"

"It travels on what we call 'a universal current,' a magnetic power found throughout the universe. That's as much as I can tell you now, Jerry. Your own scientists will be discovering it soon."

"And how did you learn to speak our language?" Jerry asked.

Ron leaned forward. "Yes, sir, how?"

Monaal laughed. "That's an easy question. I didn't have to."

"You mean people on your planet speak the same language we do?" Jerry exclaimed.

"Oh, no, we don't. Open your hand, Jerry, and look at the gismo," Monaal ordered.

Jerry uncurled his fingers and gazed in astonishment at the tiny wires on top of the gismo. They glowed cherry red. He looked up. "How come? It's not attached to anything."

"Those tiny antennae on top don't need to be. They are language converters."

"Language converters!" Jerry and Ron spoke at once.

"Yes. You see, as I speak, they convert the vibrations of my voice into sounds you are familiar with."

"Wow!" Ron whispered.

Jerry looked puzzled. "But I thought you said the gismo was a communications system from XR?"

"The bottom part is. That is why when you fastened its knobs to your circuit you were able to reach us."

Jerry gazed at the glowing wires in his hand. "And *that's* why the wires on top always turned red when we talked…they were converting the sound vibrations so we could understand each other!"

"Exactly, Jerry. You see, from our planet, Throal, we carry on trade with planets that have languages different from ours. We must be able to communicate."

"Are you going to carry on trade with our planet? Is that why you're flying around Earth?"

Monaal smiled and shook his head. "Your planet isn't ready for that yet."

"I don't see why not! We've landed on the moon already, and we'll be landing on Mars and Venus pretty soon."

"Yes, I know. But that's only the first step into space. Your inhabitants have much to learn before they're ready for interplanetary and intergalactic trade."

"Then why are you flying around Earth?" Jerry asked.

"To learn more about your continents, your oceans, your atmosphere, just as your spacemen will study other planets." Monaal held his hand out and smiled at Jerry.

Slowly Jerry handed the gismo to Monaal. "I wish I knew how to make a gismo like that myself," he sighed.

Monaal took the gismo and patted Jerry's arm. "You will, someday." He looked up at Mr. Cole. "A boy who can discover how to attach a space communication system to an improvised circuit and send messages with it will go far, I assure you!"

Mr. Cole smiled. "I hope so."

Monaal beckoned to the circle of men who clustered about him.

"We must take this to XR now," he said.

"Oh, then you found XR. Where was it?" Ron asked.

"Back on your natural satellite at crater 7, where most of our spacecraft make emergency landings." Monaal raised his hand. "Sorry, but we must go now. Good-bye, everyone." He started for the spaceship.

"Good-bye," chorused Jerry, Ron, Lou, Dodie, and Mr. Cole.

The spacemen shuffled to the silver wand and clinging to it rose slowly into the spaceship. Monaal was the last one left on the platform. He paused just below the hatch. "I'll be talking with you again, Jerry," he shouted.

"When?" Jerry called eagerly.

"When you finish making *your* gismo!" Monaal waved, and the wand disappeared into the ship. The hatch closed, the revolving fights circled faster, and the spaceship rose swiftly into the lightening sky.

Everyone stood watching it until it became a speck. Then they turned and climbed slowly back into the station wagon, whose lights had blinked on meanwhile. Mr. Cole started the car, swung it around, and headed back toward Bridgeville. No one spoke for a long time.

At last Jerry turned to his father. "You know, Dad, nobody's going to believe what happened to us tonight."

Mr. Cole nodded. "You're right."

"Maybe we'd better not mention it to anyone," Jerry said.

"A good idea, Son, we'll just keep it to ourselves. Okay, everyone?"

The sky ahead of them was turning to gold. Jerry watched it grow brighter and brighter. High above the horizon he caught the sudden glint of sunlight on metal. It lasted a moment and was gone. He would miss Monaal…but only for a while…only until he finished making a gismo of his own!

THE GISMONAUTS

For Brynne Ellen.

CHAPTER 1

June 10, 2049

Chris Cole, strapped in a forward seat of Moon Shuttle 720, tossed his red hair out of his eyes and watched the pilot and copilot. They were adjusting the vernier levers on the console—700—600—500 kilometers. The shuttle was nearing the surface of the moon.

Chris looked out the viewport at the pockmarked bleakness below, then turned toward his friend Steve Gregg, strapped in the seat next to him. Their families had lived for a long time next to each other in the satellite city of Alpha that orbited Earth.

Chris put his chin in his hands. "I wish our Scout troop had chosen Earth for an outing instead of this nothing place."

Steve grinned. "Hey, you were the one who suggested we do something different this time."

"Well, I didn't mean a boring time on the moon! I meant something exciting, like rafting down a river on Earth. My Granddad Jerry says rafting is really fun."

Steve shook his dark curly head. "Always talking about your Granddad Jerry, aren't you!"

"Sure. Why not? He's a great guy. Did I ever tell you about the time he was around our age and found a gismo—a language converter? It belonged to a little man named Monaal from the planet Throal."

"Oh, yes, that old flying saucer story of yours," Steve said, smiling.

Chris bristled. "Listen, Steve. That really happened to my granddad." He glanced at the pilot and copilot, who were speaking to each other in Swedish. "If we had that gismo here now, we could understand what our pilots are saying. The gismo converted the vibrations of a person's voice into sounds another person could understand."

"So where is the gismo now?" Steve asked.

Chris spread his hands. "The little guy Monaal—I call him a gismonaut—took it back! My granddad's been trying to make a language converter like it ever since—when he's not designing space cities. He says we could really use a gismo like that in Alpha, what with people from all over Earth living there."

"Yeah," Steve said. "Then we wouldn't have to study all those languages on our learning machines at home." He leaned forward. "Hey, look! There's the top of a moon colony!"

"Wow!" Chris exclaimed. "That must be a huge crater if a whole colony lives in it." He turned to the leader of their Boy Scout troop, Mr. Bryant, a small man with a mustache that twitched. "Is that where we're going?" Chris asked.

Mr. Bryant pointed toward an area left of the moon colony. The dark outline of a deep rille, or canyon, snaked nearby. "Right about there. That's the historic site I told you fellows about at our last meeting. Around eighty years ago, two astronauts from Earth landed there. They set up instruments to record vibrations on the moon's surface, effects of the solar winds, and other important information. They learned a lot about the moon and Earth as well."

Chris wrinkled his nose. "Sure, we learned all that stuff from the history bank. Are we just going to visit the site?"

Mr. Bryant frowned and adjusted his uniform collar. "You weren't listening very well at the last meeting, were you, Chris? I told you we have a job to do. The original landing craft's descent stage and the lunar rover have been parked right where they were left. They're a tourist attraction now. Unfortunately, a recent meteor shower hit the relics and damaged them. Our job is to collect the scattered parts of the moon rover and pick up any meteors we might find for scientific study."

Chris made a face. Under his breath he said to Steve, "Another trash collection job!" Steve grinned.

Mr. Bryant glanced anxiously around the moon shuttle at the eight Scouts strapped into their seats. They were chattering and craning their necks to get a better view of the moon. He raised his voice. "Okay, fellows, we're almost there. Now, I expect you to show me you're trustworthy Scouts in this retrieval job we've volunteered for." He eyed Chris. "It's important that we stick together when we disembark. I'll be issuing you your life-support suits, camping gear, and moontrikes."

"Moontrikes!" Chris exclaimed. "Are those anything like the electric scooters we have at home?"

"Moontrikes are three-wheelers that seat two people," Mr. Bryant said, "and they're powered by solar energy. I could only reserve five, so the troop will have to double up."

Chris whispered to Steve, "Can you picture Bryant zapping about on a trike?"

Steve giggled, and Mr. Bryant frowned at them, his mustache twitching.

The moon shuttle docked with a slight bump, and the Scouts filed out through the air locks into the domed moonport. Chris expected to feel a difference in gravity. But the moonport, attached to the moon's surface by a center rod, rotated slowly around the rod, maintaining the same gravity that Chris knew in his orbiting city of Alpha.

Mr. Bryant herded the troop through the crowd of other travelers to the baggage claim area. There he found his supply cartons, opened them, and handed out the Scouts' life-support suits, silver-colored with deep pockets all over them. The boys laughed as they climbed into the suits and connected the various hoses that would retrieve their body moisture and recycle it for their water supply. Chris found his suit surprisingly light and comfortable. He surveyed the pictures of early lunar explorers displayed on the walls of the moonport. How heavy and cumbersome those old life-support packs looked! His own pack was just twenty-five centimeters square and four centimeters thick. He hardly felt its weight at all. Much of the life-support equipment, once carried on the back, was now built into the suit itself.

The food bars Mr. Bryant distributed went into special suit pockets. Each Scout had enough for three days, he said—no snacking!

The camping gear, consisting of a space tent, shovel, and flexible pad, fitted compactly into side pockets on the moontrikes parked nearby. The moontrikes themselves were squat three-wheelers with two seats, one behind the other, on the center bar. A narrow rack ran below on each side to support the feet. On the back of each trike was a compact power system with a solar antenna, telescoped now. Levers and brakes, controlling the trike's movement, extended along the handlebars.

Mr. Bryant gave the Scouts moon maps to fit into their suit pockets. Then he explained the switches controlling the communication system built into the headgear, a transparent bubble made of a light-sensitive material that adjusted to the sun's intensity. The Scouts could always reach their leader by throwing the red switch on the headgear, he said.

"Remember, fellows, there's no air on the moon for sound waves to travel in. We'll have to rely entirely on this intercom system." He clapped his gloved hands together. "Okay, everyone!" He forced a smile. "Let's go!"

With the other Scouts, Chris and Steve wheeled their moontrike out through the air locks onto the moon's surface. What an awesome sight! The sky overhead was black. The sun shone fiercely on everything, reflecting from their headgear and making deep shadows beside their trikes as they pushed them along and extended the solar antennas. The boys laughed at their first attempts to move in adjustment with the low gravity of the moon. But before long they mastered the technique.

Then, with Mr. Bryant in the lead, the Scouts mounted their trikes and headed toward the rim of the crater surrounding the colony.

Steve drove, while Chris sat behind watching the great crater's rim grow steadily nearer. Its inner slope was fairly steep. The outer slope was more gradual, and it was fun racing down that side. Their trike's tire tracks wove back and forth, compacting the soil. Large clouds of gray dust rose slowly behind the wheels.

Once outside the crater, Mr. Bryant signaled the troop toward a distant monument rising from the flat plain. It took them half an hour to reach it. Chris realized that the lack of atmosphere on the moon made distances deceptive; things looked much closer than they were.

Even before they reached the monument, Chris could see bits of the old descent module and the lunar rover scattered about the moonscape. He frowned. Why was it that Boy Scouts were always tapped to clean up after picnics, festivals, or Scout fairs? Now it was after a meteor shower on the moon!

On reaching the historical monument, the boys dismounted and received their collection bags and last-minute instructions. Mr. Bryant handed each pair of Scouts a sectioned-off map of the area. He had written the names of two Scouts in each wedge-shaped section. Chris noticed that he and Steve had been assigned to an area bordered by the deep rille he had seen from the moon shuttle.

"The area that you and Steve are to cover," Mr. Bryant told Chris, "is a good distance from here, but some meteors have been sighted there. Whatever you do, don't go down into the rille. That's off limits to us."

"What if we see a big meteor in the rille?" Chris asked.

"Don't touch it!" Mr. Bryant's mustache twitched. "That rille has been designated a dangerous area. Stay out of it!" He addressed the rest of the troop. "I don't need to tell you fellows to move carefully. There's a delayed-action phenomenon in this low gravity that can throw things off balance. Remember, too, there'll be no darkness on this section of the moon for the next three days. You're all wearing watches. Keep track of your time and take a rest every twelve hours or so. In three days—that's this coming Friday—we'll meet back here with our collections. If you miss us here, return to the moonport. The shuttle to Alpha leaves at 6:00 p.m. Be back early. And don't forget the red switch on your intercom. It's a hot line to me. Any questions?"

There were none.

"Okay, you're on your own!" Mr. Bryant waved his arm toward the horizon. "Move out!"

Chris stuffed his and Steve's collection bags behind their camping gear on the moon-trike. Steve mounted the driver's seat. He grinned at Chris. "When I get tired, you can drive."

"Yeah? Fat chance you'll get tired." Actually, Chris didn't mind riding behind for a while. He could study the moonscape. There was something both beautiful and frightening about it. But what could be so dangerous about an old rille? Chris wondered.

He and Steve could never have guessed!

CHAPTER 2

The Rille

Chris and Steve headed toward their assigned area. They passed great domes and craters of smooth gray-tan moon soil. The inviting hill-climb slopes were more than Steve could resist.

"Here we go," he shouted. "Hang on!" He drove the trike up the slanting side of a crater, then turned and raced down to level ground.

After the third time, Chris tapped Steve on the headgear. "Look, this is fun, but we'd better stick to the map and head for the rille."

"You want to drive?" Steve said. "Here, go ahead and try it." He dismounted.

Chris took over the driver's seat, and Steve climbed onto the seat behind him. Carefully Chris drove around a small crater and a couple of boulders. He began to feel the response of the trike. It was great! Another smooth slope of a dome beckoned. One more hill-climb wouldn't hurt. He urged the trike up the slope, slid around, and started to dash down again, a cloud of moon dust behind him.

"Watch out!" Steve called, but he was too late. A pile of moon rocks the size of basketballs appeared abruptly in their path. The trike hit the rocks, and the boys bounced off in slow motion. They fell in the dust, while the trike sailed into the air. It landed on its wheels and ran on, disappearing behind the slope of another crater.

Chris sat up and looked over at Steve, who was rising slowly to his feet. "You okay, Steve?" he asked over the intercom.

"I guess so," Steve said. "It sure feels funny to walk." He took several bouncing steps.

Chris stood up. He found he could move easier if he hopped along one foot ahead of the other. "Hey, Steve, this is a neat way to travel. Come on. We've got to find the trike."

It was easy to follow the trike's tire tracks in the dust. The tracks ended at a small crater two meters across, with deep shadows in the bottom.

"Where did it go?" Steve asked. "There aren't any tracks on the other side."

"It must be in here," Chris said, peering into the intense blackness inside the crater. He spotted a section of the trike's wheel barely showing in the sun. "It's here, all right," he said and then hopped down into the crater to pull the trike out. The solar antenna was bent to one side.

Anxiously he and Steve bent it back. After a few minutes of adjustment, the trike started again.

Chris sighed with relief. "I guess you'd better drive. I'm not too hot at it."

Steve grinned through his headgear. "You're okay on the straight and level stuff." He slung a leg over the driver's seat. "Only lay off the hill-climbs. Okay?"

Chris grinned back. "That goes for you, too, buddy. We'd better stop fooling around and locate that rille."

It was hard to figure out from the map just which crater and dome were the ones they were passing. From the map grids, however, Chris finally recognized a crater just before the rille. "I think we're getting there," he said.

They rounded the crater's cone. A sinuous black shadow sliced across the moonscape.

"Here it is," Chris said.

Steve barely stopped in time.

The boys climbed off the trike. They were standing near the edge of a canyon hundreds of meters deep. The black shadow lay on the opposite wall. Below them, the steep rille sides were composed of gray soil and loose rocks. Steve kicked a small rock over the edge. It rolled silently down, down, disappearing into the blackness at the bottom.

"Wow!" Steve exclaimed. "That's plenty deep."

Chris nodded. "I see why it's off limits." He turned back to the trike. "Well, I guess we'd better start the trash pickup." He yanked at the collection bags he had tucked behind the camping gear. The sudden motion raised the trike from the ground, releasing the brake. Slowly the trike began to roll toward the canyon edge.

"Grab it, Steve! Grab it!" Chris shouted over the intercom.

Steve turned and reached for the handlebars. He managed to seize them, but the momentum of the trike carried him along with it. To Chris's horror, Steve and the trike disappeared over the edge of the rille.

Chris ran to the edge. In a shower of fine soil, Steve and the trike were sliding in slow motion down the steep slope. "Steve! Steve!" Chris called over the intercom.

But all he heard was a faint "Whoah!" Then silence. With a sickening knot in his stomach, Chris watched his friend and the trike grow smaller and smaller, until swallowed at last in the black shadows far below.

Even though the rille was off limits, Chris knew he must go after Steve. He hesitated. Should he notify Mr. Bryant over the intercom first? No, better not. It was his own carelessness that had caused the accident. He should have remembered what Mr. Bryant said about moving deliberately—not yanking at things. Besides, Steve might be hurt and need Chris's help immediately.

Chris eased himself over the edge of the rille and took a big breath as he let go. He felt himself start to slide, slowly at first, then faster. The soil and small rocks flowed along with him. There was no way to stop himself in this slow-motion avalanche.

The blackness below grew closer and closer. The sides of the rille narrowed in on him as he neared the bottom. He felt himself slowing down at last. He slid into the shadow. One of his feet hit something soft that gave. He jerked his foot back. Whatever it was moved slowly to one side. Chris felt his heart thump loudly. He peered into the gloom, then laughed with relief. It was Steve!

"Are you okay?" Chris asked anxiously over the intercom.

He saw Steve's bubble headgear nod slowly. "Yes, I guess so. What are *you* doing down here?"

"I thought you might be hurt and need help."

"I'm not hurt, but I sure could use some help getting out of here. We've got to find that stupid trike first, though. Can you see it?" He rose slowly to his feet. "It's murder to find anything in these moon shadows."

Chris stood up too. Even by the reflected light from the sunlit slope he had just descended, Chris couldn't see beyond an arm's length. The light screen in his transparent headgear was slow to adjust to the dimness. He bumped into Steve as they searched for the trike.

"Look, Steve," Chris said, "maybe it ran along the bottom of the rille the way it did before."

"Yeah." Steve nodded. "It was turning end over end in front of me. It reached the bottom before I did. It could have landed on its wheels."

Chris touched Steve's arm and pointed. "There's a sharp curve in the rille up ahead. Maybe the trike went in that direction."

"If it did, it would have run into the opposite wall and slowed down," Steve said, starting toward the curve. "We've got to find those wheels before we try climbing out of here." They rounded the curve, and Chris stopped suddenly. "Look!" He pointed at a gigantic boulder jutting out of the sunlit slope of the rille. There was an opening below it wide enough for the moon shuttle to enter.

"Wow!" Steve exclaimed. "A cave! I didn't know there were caves on the moon."

Chris loped toward it. "Looks to me like a mining tunnel, only a lot bigger. Do you suppose this is why the rille is off limits?"

"Could be. Maybe the government is mining some secret stuff out of here."

Chris stopped and looked back. "If the trike had rolled along the rille floor and hit the wall over there"—he pointed—"it would have ricocheted in this direction, right into that cave. Come on. Let's look inside."

Cautiously they entered the opening. Surprisingly, the shadows weren't as dark inside as outside. A phosphorescent glow radiated from the walls and ceiling, which appeared smooth like the inside of a tube. The floor was composed of some odd springy material, not like the moon soil they had been traveling on.

Chris was right about the trike. It had ricocheted four or five meters inside the opening and was lying on its side.

Steve hurried over and stood it on its wheels. "Wouldn't you know! The antenna is bent again."

Chris joined him. "What about the camping gear? Is it still okay?" He bent over to examine it, then straightened and looked at Steve. "Do you feel something funny?"

"Like what?"

"Like we're moving?"

Steve looked around. "Yeah! Like the ground is moving under us. Hey, we'd better get out of here!" He began rolling the trike toward the opening.

Chris followed. He was soon aware, however, that they were no closer to the opening than when they started. The ground beneath them, like a conveyor belt, was carrying them deeper into the tunnel.

The hair began to rise on the back of Chris's neck. "Quick, Steve, hurry!" He joined his partner, and together they pushed the trike as fast as they could, but it was a losing battle. Despite their efforts, they were no closer to the opening than before.

Chris watched in dismay as the tunnel entrance grew smaller and smaller.

CHAPTER 3

Intergalactic Way Station

Steve, panting from the exertion of running with the trike, looked over at Chris. "We'll never make it out of here!"

"Push faster," Chris gasped.

"I *am* pushing as fast as I can. This is getting us nowhere. I feel like a gerbil in a wheel. Let's stop."

Chris slowed down. "Okay. I'd better contact Mr. Bryant." He flipped the red switch up, but only static filled his headgear. There was no answering voice.

Steve let go of the trike. "You won't reach anyone from in here." He waved his hands at the tunnel walls. "Radio signals can't travel through rock like that."

Steve was right. Chris turned the red switch off. His knees felt suddenly weak, and he sat down on the tunnel floor. He could definitely feel the movement now. It felt like a conveyor belt, something man-made. What for?

He turned to Steve. "Where do you suppose we're going?"

"Going!" Steve sat down beside Chris. "Are you crazy? We aren't going anywhere!"

"I didn't mean that. Where do you suppose this tunnel floor is taking us? It's got to end somewhere."

Steve shrugged. "Like a dump, maybe?"

"What about a mine shaft? Somebody built this for a reason. We know there are mines on the moon."

"Hey, yeah!" Steve sounded a bit cheerful. "Maybe we can get out through the other end. Too bad we don't know where the conveyor switches are so we could reverse this belt."

Chris peered toward the inner end of the tunnel. He jumped to his feet. "Look! There's the end!"

Steve rose and stared into the dimness ahead. "Looks like a big door of some kind, doesn't it?"

"Sure does, but it's closed."

As they neared the door, Chris could see it was made of shiny metal and filled the entire opening. When they were within four meters, a crack of light appeared down the center. Silently the two halves of the door separated, sliding into the tunnel walls.

The two boys entered a cavernous room larger than the moonport they had arrived at earlier. The floor beneath their feet stopped moving. As Chris's headgear adjusted to the light, he saw a single panel glowing in the ceiling. Directly below it, a circular spacecraft rested on retractable legs. A ladder led up into it. In the dimness of the opposite wall, a small door was visible. No one seemed to be about.

Steve looked around slowly. "This is no mine, Chris."

"Looks like a hangar of some kind." Chris snapped his fingers. "I've got it. They fly into the tunnel, activate a photoelectric eye, and the floor brings them in here." He glanced about in the gloom at the doorway they had just entered. Its two halves were sliding together again.

"Yeah," Steve said. "We must have crossed the light beam when we entered the tunnel. But that spaceship doesn't look like any I've seen before. Maybe it's an experimental craft the government doesn't want anyone to know about."

"Oh-oh," Chris said. "*That's* why the rille is off limits. Now we're in real trouble!"

Steve turned toward the tunnel door. "Look. Before anyone sees us here, maybe we can locate the gadget that activates the tunnel floor to go the other way. That spacecraft must go out as well as come in."

"Sure, but how do we get the door to open?"

"The same way it opened before—photoelectric eye. Do you see one anywhere?"

The boys hunted in the gloom for a light beam or switch that would trigger the door. They found none.

"Well," Chris said at last, "we'll have to go through that smaller door over there and ask someone to let us out. Might as well leave the trike here. We'll be coming back this way."

They crossed the wide floor. The smaller door slid open, and they found themselves in a long alleyway with doors on both sides. Hardly had they entered when a guard, slightly over a meter tall, emerged from one of the doorways. He wore a tight-fitting one-piece suit of dark blue with a red collar and belt. A small rectangle, the size of a domino, hung from a thong around his neck. He motioned the boys to remove their headgear.

Steve looked at Chris. "Should we?"

"Why not? If he can breathe in here without one, so can we."

They removed their headgear. They had no difficulty in breathing.

The guard said in a high voice, "May I ask what you are doing here?"

Chris waved his hand toward the doorway they had entered. "We were looking for our moontrike in that tunnel back there, and the floor started moving and—"

"Come with me." The guard beckoned for them to follow. They entered an elevator that whisked them downward. It stopped, and they followed the guard to a door. He knocked.

"Come in," another high-pitched voice ordered.

They entered. The carpeted room had a large low desk in the center with a row of communication buttons across it. Several chairs stood in front of the desk. Behind it, a battery of controls and three-dimensional screens lined the wall. To one side, a large transparent map marked with grid lines and clusters of colored disks was suspended from the ceiling.

Another small man, dressed like the first, sat behind the desk. "Yes?"

"Sir," the guard said, "these beings penetrated to Hangar One alleyway."

The second man rose and waved the guard out of the room. His face was stern as he looked at the boys. "Where are you from?"

Chris looked questioningly at Steve, then back at the small man. "We're from the satellite city Alpha that orbits Earth."

"Ah." The man's face relaxed. "Earthlings! May I ask what you are doing here?"

"Well, you see, sir," Chris began again, "we were looking for our moontrike in that tunnel, and the floor started moving and brought us into that Hangar One, as your guard called it."

"Moontrike? Oh, yes." The man nodded briefly.

Steve tried to explain. "You see, mister, our Scout troop is here to help recover pieces of that historic lunar rover and descent module that were damaged by a meteor shower. We'd appreciate it if you'd show us how to get out of here."

"Please sit down," the man said.

Chris and Steve obeyed.

The man shook his head apologetically. "I'm afraid you cannot leave," he said.

Chris and Steve looked at each other in speechless surprise. Then Chris spoke. "Listen, if it's because of that experimental spacecraft the government is working on, don't worry. We won't tell anybody about it. Honest."

"Experimental spacecraft?" The man smiled. "That ship is far from being experimental. It belongs to a member of the Intergalactic Federation. We maintain this way station here inside the moon. Your government knows nothing about it—and must not know."

Steve looked incredulous. "Intergalactic! You mean you're from outer space?"

The man nodded.

"But why can't our government know?" Chris asked.

"It would bring about a confrontation we wish to avoid for the time being." He paused. "You see, we hope someday to invite the Earth government to join us, but your leaders haven't proved them-selves ready yet."

Chris leaned forward. "I don't see why not. My granddad says we've come a long way in just the last seventy years. We've managed to bring all the countries together so they're not fighting each other anymore. We've sent out all kinds of probes and manned spacecraft to the planets in our solar system. Our orbiting satellite cities are making it possible to reduce Earth's population and pollution so we can have clean rivers and clean air again. How can you say we aren't ready?"

The man smiled. "You have indeed come a long way. There are a few things, however, you must change, such as the attitude that you *own* all the planets and moons in this solar system. They are not the property of any one planet, but are provided for all beings to use and enjoy. When your government comes to this and other realizations, then Earth will be ready to join the Intergalactic Federation. For now, however, I'm sorry. I cannot let you leave here."

"But, sir—" Chris began, his eyes filling with fear.

The man held up his hand. "Don't be frightened, my boy. No one here will harm you. And since we have much time together ahead of us, let me introduce myself. I am Monaal."

CHAPTER 4

Monaal

Chris looked at Steve for a moment, then stared at Monaal. "Are—are you from the planet Throal?"

Monaal looked startled. "Why, yes. How did you know?"

"My granddad told me about you." Chris pointed at the red glowing rectangle hanging from a thong around Monaal's neck. "That must be a gismo—I mean a language converter, like the one my granddad found."

Monaal stroked the tiny fur-like wires that covered the top of the gismo like a brush. "Yes, this is a language converter." Suddenly his face brightened. "Why, of course! It happened seventy years ago. The boy named Jerry Cole. He found one of these on the planet Earth. I remember he, too, called it a gismo when he returned it to me."

Chris smiled triumphantly at Steve. "See? I told you it really did happen to my granddad!"

Monaal pointed at Chris. "You are Jerry's grandson?"

"Yes, I'm Christopher Cole—Chris to everyone. And this is Steve Gregg."

Monaal nodded at Steve, then returned to Chris. "How *is* your grandfather? I understand aging on Earth has been slowed."

"Granddad's fine. He's middle-aged—in his eighties—and designs satellite cities like Alpha, where we live."

Monaal nodded, smiling. "I knew Jerry would do something constructive. He was a remarkable boy—hooking up the converter to an improvised circuit and sending messages to me.

Chris rose. "Look, Mr. Monaal, now that you know who I am, couldn't you let us go?"

Monaal turned. "Come with me." He led the way from the room. The boys followed.

Chris leaned close to Steve. "This is a real break. I didn't think leaving would be this easy."

"Me neither," Steve whispered. Then he stopped suddenly, and his face fell. "Our trike! We forgot to get it." He moved closer to Monaal. "Please, Mr. Monaal, we'll have to go back for our moontrike. We left it in Hangar One."

"You won't be needing it," Monaal said.

Steve, puzzled, looked at Chris as they followed Monaal.

Monaal opened a door and motioned them in. The room reminded Chris of the gym locker rooms at the recreation center in Alpha. There were long closed cabinets around the walls, with benches in the middle of the room.

Monaal waved at the benches. "You may change here."

"But why?" Chris asked. "If we're going outside again, we'll need these life-support suits."

"You won't be needing them in here," Monaal said and opened a locker. He drew out two pairs of blue coveralls like the ones he was wearing.

Chris wrinkled his forehead. "Aren't you taking us back to the moon's surface?"

"No, I'm sorry."

"But, sir!" Chris's voice was full of disappointment. "Now that you know who I am and about my granddad and all, aren't you going to trust me? I promised I wouldn't say a word to anyone about this place, and I meant it!"

"Me too," Steve added. "I won't tell anyone either."

Monaal smiled at them. "I can't be sure of that. I need to study you further. You may be able to leave later, but on one condition."

"What's that?" Chris asked.

"Prove to me that you can be trusted."

Chris spread his hands in front of him. "Isn't our word good enough?"

Monaal shook his head. "Words are easily forgotten. Actions are not."

"What can we do?" Chris asked.

Monaal held out the coveralls. "Put these on, and I'll tell you."

Quickly the boys began removing their life-support suits.

Monaal sat on a bench as he talked. "There are beings from many worlds in our Intergalactic Federation. Over eons of time, we have learned to work together, to treat one another as equals, and to trust one another. Those using this way station are here to rest, to repair their spacecraft, or to help with the station's operation. If you show me that you can work in harmony with these beings, that you regard them as your equals, that you trust them and can be trusted in return, then you may leave."

Chris zipped up the blue coveralls. "That won't be hard. We've learned to do that in our satellite city."

"Sure," Steve said. "People from all over Earth live there, and we get along fine."

Monaal nodded. "Good. Then it shouldn't be difficult to work with Gat. He's from the planet Felson in the galaxy of Brood. He's in charge of all personnel here and fills in where needed. Right now he's at the console controlling craft entry in our main hangar. Come. I'll take you to him."

As they left the room, Steve whispered to Chris, "Now we'll find out how to open that door and reverse the tunnel floor."

But instead of returning as they had come, Monaal led them to a small cylinder-shaped conveyance that fit into a horizontal tube in the wall. They entered the capsule, shut the door, and felt themselves sucked through the tube at great speed. The ride ended in another hangar many times larger than the first.

Chris could hardly believe his eyes. Enormous spacecraft—some elongated tubes, some saucer-shaped with transparent domes on top—were parked everywhere.

On one side of the hangar wall was a giant door. It was slowly opening. On a platform nearby stood a console covered with switches and buttons and colored lights. A small dark figure was operating the controls. Lights of blue, green, lavender, red, pink, and yellow flashed on and off on the console.

The door opened fully, and Chris saw a huge round spacecraft float silently in, attached by a line to a midget tow car, also round in shape, with a red dome on top. Chris smiled to himself. It looked like a ladybug leading a huge turtle by a leash. The midget car maneuvered the spacecraft into a vacant stall, pushing and tugging by turn.

Monaal pointed. "That craft has just arrived from the planet Hummo. You can tell by the emblem underneath—that *H* with a dissecting line on the center bar."

"Wow!" Steve exclaimed. "I've never seen a spacecraft that big!"

Chris looked puzzled. "How come our moon colonies never report seeing these ships arrive?"

Monaal smiled. "Because they approach the back side of the moon, the side you never see from Earth, and you have no colonies there as yet."

"You mean we're clear on the other side of the moon right now?" Chris asked incredulously. "How could we get here so fast?"

"Through the gas-belt tunnels left when the moon's volcanoes cooled," Monaal said.

"You mean there are hollow places in the moon?" Steve asked.

Monaal nodded. "Lots of them. Your seismic detectors should have noticed that."

Chris grinned. "This is crazy. Our scientists say the moon is solid."

"Let them think so," Monaal said with a chuckle. "That way they won't disturb our intergalactic way station."

Chris looked puzzled. "But what about that Hangar One we came through? Don't you use that too?"

"Very seldom. It was built long ago, before your moon colonies were established. Its entrance is too easily detected. For this reason, we set up a radioactive belt along the rille to discourage investigation. That's why your government declared the area off limits, even though the belt is no longer active. Only a few small craft that can fly low inside the rille use Hangar One now." He started toward the console. "But come. I want you to meet Gat."

They crossed to the console platform. "Gat?" Monaal called. "Could you come down here, please?"

"Just a minute," a gruff voice answered. Chris heard several clicks of buttons and switches, a command that someone "take over here," and then a scurry of feet. A shaggy figure leaped suddenly from the platform and landed in front of them. Chris stepped back in astonishment. The being, no taller than Monaal, was covered from head to foot with coarse black hair. His ears were large, and his green eyes, in a small wizened face, were narrow and piercing. The gismo hanging about his thick neck was almost hidden in the fur on his broad chest. His arms were long, his hands reaching below his knees.

"What do you want?" he rumbled.

"I have two new workers for you to train, Gat—these beings, Chris and Steve. They are Earthlings."

"Earthlings, eh?" Gat cocked his head and stared at the boys. "I thought Earthlings were taller than that."

Chris shuffled. "Well, grown-up Earthlings are. We're still kids."

Gat raised his bushy eyebrows. "Children?" He looked at Monaal.

"I'm afraid so," Monaal said. "Be sure they are warned about the Jovan craft. These two are here accidentally, of course. If they wish to leave, they must prove themselves trustworthy."

Gat held out a hairy hand to Chris. "Then I'll see that they do." His narrow green eyes drilled into Chris's blue ones.

Chris shivered. He felt an instant uneasiness with this strange-looking being. Hesitantly he reached for the extended hand and winced. Where fingers should have been, there were claws!

CHAPTER 5

Escape from Gat

With a claw, Gat beckoned the boys to follow him. Chris glanced at Steve. It was evident that Steve felt as bothered as he did by this hairy being whose rolling gait reminded Chris of a chimpanzee. Gat led them to an alcove nearby, where a fleet of the circular midget cars was parked.

He pointed. "These are piloteers. We use them to bring the spacecraft into the hangar, as you noticed. They're powered by storage cells."

Steve bent over to look at them. "Where are the wheels?"

"They have none. They move on a cushion of air formed by jets in the bottom of the craft. Your job will be to go outside with one of these tugs, hook onto the lead line of an incoming ship, and draw it into the hangar." He walked over to a piloteer and pushed a button on its side. The top swung back like a hinged lid.

Gat motioned the boys to climb into the two formfitting seats facing the dashboard. He leaped in behind them, reached over with a hairy arm, and touched a switch. The top closed with a snap, and a small light on the dash glowed red. Chris could hear a strange hissing sound and looked questioningly at Gat.

"The piloteer is pressurizing," Gat said, "so we can go outside on the moon's surface to pick up the ships."

Gat gave the boys detailed instructions on how to operate the piloteer, and after several questions and a few practice flights, both were able to fly the little craft about the hangar, a few centimeters above the floor.

Steve grinned at Chris. "This is more fun than the moontrike!"

Chris nodded, but thought to himself, If only we didn't have to work under this weird guy that sounds like a human being but looks like an animal.

Gat directed them through the hangar entrance and along a cavernous tunnel to another monstrous door. It opened at a remote signal from a switch inside the piloteer.

Chris and Steve found themselves out on the surface of the moon. It was dark, and as Chris's eyes adjusted to the dimness, he stared in amazement at the skyline. They were in the deep bowl of a massive crater. The stars above shone steadily, and as he watched, one star detached itself and grew larger and larger. Rapid conversation passed between Gat and the incoming craft. A moment later, red, blue, and green lights, circling the perimeter of the ship, reflected on the crater with a whirling band of color. Chris felt slightly dizzy watching the pinwheeling rainbow.

The bright glow from the bottom of the craft vanished. Gat flashed a spotlight on the emblem—three concentric circles—emblazoned on the underside of the ship. "Never," he said gruffly, "attach to a craft displaying the letter J with a spear through it."

"Why not?" Chris asked.

"It's the emblem of Jovan craft, and this way station is off limits to them."

A signal flashed from the craft above, and Gat showed Chris how to signal back. A silver-colored line descended in a column of light and reached out toward the piloteer. Chris, under Gat's direction, pressed a button that released a slender hook. It fastened onto the craft's line. Steve drove back into the tunnel, with Gat barking directions.

Chris watched the spacecraft float silently behind them. "Can't those ships come in here on their own power?"

Gat shook his shaggy head. "Hot gases form around these craft as they're propelled. Should the ships come in on their own power, the gases could collect in the tunnel and hangar and become dangerous." He directed Steve to pull the craft into a vacant space within the hangar.

Chris wished he could stay and watch the beings from the arriving craft disembark. But a green light flashed on the hangar's console, signaling that a big spaceship wished to leave. Gat ordered Steve to pick it up.

Following a second trip to the deep crater and back, Gat opened the piloteer and leaped out. "You are on your own, Earthlings. Watch the lights on the console. In your particular piloteer, blue flashing means you are to pick up a craft outside. Green means a craft in here is ready to leave. Pay no attention to the lights for the other piloteers. And remember, no ships from Jovan!"

Another blue light began flashing on the console, and Steve spun the piloteer around, signaled the door to open, and raced down the tunnel. "Man! This is fantastic!" he exclaimed. "Wait till we tell the kids back home about this. They won't believe us."

"They'd *better* not!" Chris said, grinning. "We're not supposed to tell anybody about it, remember?"

Steve shrugged. "Yeah, yeah, but who's to know?"

"Monaal, when all those Earthling friends of ours begin landing shuttles in that crater out there."

Steve chuckled.

Chris, handling the hooking and unhooking, still wished he could stop long enough to see what the beings coming here from other galaxies looked like. He peered at the drivers of the other piloteers scurrying about as their signal lights flashed on the big console. He knew the other drivers must be small to fit into the piloteers. One was a girl, he was sure. She had long dark hair, and she smiled at him as she zapped by to answer a flashing red light for her piloteer. He wished he could meet her.

Why, he wondered, were there so few beings from the Intergalactic Federation around? Were they hiding because uninvited Earthlings were in the way station? Well, if he had his way, he wouldn't be messing around this unfriendly place. He'd be out on the moon's surface where he belonged! Another blue light flashed on the console.

Steve and Chris were kept busy as spacecraft after spacecraft entered and left the way station. Steve, at last, leaned back against the headrest of his bucket seat. "Say, I'm getting tired!"

"So am I, and hungry too. Gat sure doesn't believe in nutrition breaks, or whatever they call them here."

Steve leaned forward. "Maybe if we pretend that there's something wrong with this piloteer, we can stop for a while."

"Good idea. Let's return to the alcove."

Steve drove hesitantly to the parking area.

He pushed the release button. The top flipped open, and the boys climbed out stiffly. They stretched.

A piloteer came scurrying along and stopped beside them.

"Oh-oh," Steve said. "Trouble."

The top swung open on the other car, and Chris saw the smiling girl he had glimpsed earlier. She vaulted out of her piloteer.

"Hi," she said, tossing her long dark hair over her shoulders. She was no taller than Monaal and dressed in the same style of blue coveralls. The gismo she wore glowed red as she spoke. "You must be the Earthlings my father told me about."

Chris raised his eyebrows. "Are you Monaal's daughter?"

"Yes. My name is Kaali."

"Hey!" Chris exclaimed. "I've heard that name before. My Great-Aunt Dodie mentioned it."

"How did she know it?" Kaali looked surprised. "Where did she hear about me?"

Chris grinned. "From your dad. It was a long time ago, when my granddad found a gismo and talked with Monaal."

"I must have been very young then."

"You were. How come you're not as old as my great-aunt now? She's about eighty."

"So am I," Kaali said.

"Eighty! You look more like thirteen."

Kaali laughed. "On Throal, people don't age the way Earthlings do. We live a very long time."

"Yeah, Monaal told my Great-Aunt Dodie he was seven hundred years old by the calendar on Throal, and that was over seventy years ago!"

"Wow!" Steve said. "You Throalians must live forever!"

"Not quite," Kaali said with a smile. "But tell me. Why are you leaving your piloteer?"

Steve leaned against the car. "We're tired."

"And hungry too," Chris added. "I wish we could get at the food in the pockets of our life-support suits."

"Yeah," Steve said. "The suits are in a locker way off somewhere near that other hangar that's not used much."

"I know which room you mean," Kaali said. "Come. I'll take you there."

Chris motioned toward the console. "What about Gat? He might get mad if we up and walked out on him."

Kaali grinned. "Just tell him that you're taking a break. He won't mind. Gat's a very nice person."

Chris started toward the console. "He doesn't look that way to me. He scares me the way he scowls."

"You don't know Gat. That scowl is put on to cover up his soft heart. You'll really like him once you get to know him."

Kaali was right about one thing. When Chris asked if they might take a break, Gat agreed curtly.

With Kaali leading, the boys were soon back in the locker room rummaging for food in their life-support suits. Kaali left to talk to her father.

On seeing his suit again, Chris wished more than ever that he could climb into it and leave the way station with its strange-looking beings. Suddenly he had an idea. He leaned close to Steve and spoke softly. "Listen, I think I know how we can get out of this place."

Steve munched on a space food bar. "How?"

"With our piloteer. After we release a spacecraft out there on the moon, we won't bother to come back. Instead, we'll cut out of the crater. It's dark. No one will see us."

Steve reached for another food bar. "Are you crazy? We'd never find our way around all those mountains and craters out there. Have you ever seen a map of the far side of the moon?"

"Sure, I have." Chris reached into one of the knee pockets of his life-support suit and drew out a map. "Remember? Mr. Bryant gave these to us." He slipped it into a coverall pocket. "Once we figure out on this map where we are, it will be a cinch to drive to a moon colony. Those piloteers can zoom. We should be able to make it to the bright side of the moon in no time!"

Steve looked doubtful. "Those piloteers might not operate for long distances out on the moon's surface."

"Why not? They've got storage cells that hold a charge for a long time. Gat said so. Since they're pressurized for the moon's surface, we'd be okay until we got to a colony." Chris reached for his suit. "Better stuff all the food you can into your coverall pockets."

Steve hesitated. "You're sure it will work?"

"Sure, I'm sure!"

The boys stuffed their pockets with food. Kaali returned, and within minutes they were back inside their piloteer following orders flashed to them from the console. They released a departing craft and watched it speed away into the black sky.

"Now!" Chris said. "Let's get out of here!"

"Which way?" Steve asked.

"Straight up over the crater's edge."

Steve headed for the dim outline in the distance. The piloteer sped across the flat floor of the crater. Chris kept glancing back to see whether anyone was following them. All he could see was the starlight glinting on the metal door.

The inner wall of the crater was steep. The piloteer labored as Steve urged it upward. They reached the rim at last.

Steve stopped the car for a moment. *"Now* which way?"

Chris studied the dark rugged moonscape, then the map on his lap. He was about to answer when a high whining filled his ears. A small domed spacecraft shot out from the airlock door. In a moment, it hovered over their piloteer. Chris felt a jolt as the spacecraft, like a magnet, drew the piloteer up and all but swallowed it. Within seconds, both the bigger and the smaller craft were headed back toward the hangar.

Steve looked at Chris in disgust. "You and your bright ideas!" he said. *"Now* we'll get it!"

CHAPTER 6

Off to the Mines

The spacecraft, with the piloteer attached beneath it, reentered the air lock. It didn't release the tow car until it was inside the great hangar and the doors were closed. Monaal and Gat appeared beside the car.

Steve looked at Chris. "What are we going to tell them?"

Chris shrugged. "The truth, I guess—that we wanted to get out of here."

Steve snorted. "Listen, stupid, don't you think they've figured that out already?" He leaned over and pressed the top-release button. The piloteer swung open.

Chris smiled sheepishly as he and Steve climbed out. His smile faded, however, at the stern expressions on Gat's and Monaal's faces. No one spoke as the boys, their eyes on the hangar floor, shuffled uncomfortably.

Monaal spoke at last. "Trustworthy, eh?"

Chris glanced up, then down. "Look, Mr. Monaal, we weren't going to tell anyone about this place, honest." He looked into Monaal's eyes. "But we *had* to leave. Our Scoutmaster, Mr. Bryant, is out there wondering what's happened to us. He's probably looking for us right now."

"No doubt," Monaal said dryly. "You were very foolish to think you could survive out there on that rugged terrain."

"But the piloteer is pressurized," Chris said, "and has a power cell."

"It would work for only a short while," Monaal replied. "Once it was out of range of this station, it would lose all its power. I had you brought back here for your own safety, as well as for ours. Your conduct forces me to assign you to a more secure place." He turned. "Follow me."

Chris and Steve, with Gat in the rear, trudged after Monaal.

What was going to happen to them? Chris wondered. Were they being led off to prison? He should have known that escaping from a super-intelligent being like Monaal would be impossible. Had Kaali alerted her father? She didn't seem like that kind of person. Still, all beings in the Intergalactic Federation were bound to keep their way station a secret from Earthlings.

They entered another tube capsule that whisked them deep within the moon. When it stopped at last, Monaal motioned the boys out. They were in a room full of whining machinery. Throalians, like Monaal, were scurrying about.

Monaal led them to a door at the far end of the room. He faced the boys. "This is a mine. We are extracting talonium ore from the moon's interior. It is fed into the machines you see here, refined, and turned into the strong metal we use to make and repair our spacecraft. Talonium is a rare substance found only in the interiors of moons."

"So *that's* why so many spaceships come here—for the metal," Chris said.

"That is one reason," Monaal agreed. "Earth engineers haven't discovered talonium yet. When they do, they'll be able to build ships strong and light enough for intergalactic travel."

Steve wrinkled his forehead. "You mean our scientists don't know all the metals yet?"

"No, not yet. They, like the rest of us in the universe, are constantly discovering new things. Some of us, of course, are further ahead in this discovery than others. But come." Monaal opened the door. "Gat will show you your tasks here."

They entered the mine. Though the passage was wide, it was not much higher than Chris and Steve. The tunnel, Chris decided, was made for Throalians. The floors and walls of the mine appeared to be hard rock with a metallic glint. The ceiling glowed with the same phosphorescent light that Chris remembered in the entry tunnel. A long conveyor belt stretched the length of the passageway.

The air grew warmer the farther back they walked. Smaller passageways led off from the main one, and Chris could hear machinery rumbling in them. Since he had lived in a satellite city all his life, he knew little about mines—only what he had read on his learning machine at home. He wondered how advanced the mining operations would be here.

Monaal stopped at last near a small passageway. "Gat will take you from here and assign your work. I must return." His eyes probed Chris's face. "Your work here will be hard, but not beyond your ability. I'm sorry we have to put you here. When Gat assures me you can be trusted, then, and only then, can we discuss your return to the moon's surface."

Monaal left.

Gat beckoned the boys to follow him down the narrower tunnel. At the end of it, small noisy machines run by Throalians augered into the rock. The sound ricocheted between the walls. Buckets on a belt carried the ore to a hopper on tracks that led out of the tunnel. Chris gazed in surprise. This method of mining was even more primitive than those used on Earth, if he were to believe his learning machine.

With a wave of his hairy arm, Gat silenced the Throalians' machines. Chris welcomed the brief quiet. Gat pointed toward the hopper. "You Earthlings are strong. When this is full of ore, push it to the main tunnel, dump it onto the conveyor belt, and return." He signaled the miners to continue, surveyed the work for a time, and then left.

It took the boys' combined strength to push the loaded hopper to the main tunnel.

"Whew!" Steve panted. "This is like the Middle Ages!"

"Yes, like the old salt mines." Chris stopped to wipe the sweat from his forehead. "I guess we had it coming to us, though. I really blew it on that escape attempt. How was I to know the piloteer would die on us?"

Steve leaned against the tunnel wall. "When we climbed out of the car, I expected Gat to jump down our throats. But he didn't say a word. Notice?"

"Yes. I thought he'd go after us with those mean-looking claws of his, but he didn't."

Steve put his back against the hopper and pushed backward. "It was Monaal who ripped into us instead."

Chris pushed with his shoulders. "Let's face it, Steve. We could have ended up out there like a couple of dead bugs in a matchbox. It didn't have to matter to anyone here. 'Dead men tell no tales,' they say, so why did Monaal bring us back?"

"Maybe, as he said, to save our lives." Steve shook his head. "This whole setup is weird. I feel like some guy in an old folktale having to prove I'm worthy of the princess." He dumped the contents of the hopper onto the conveyor.

Chris grinned. "Speaking of princesses, isn't that Kaali coming this way?"

It was. She stopped to chat with various workers. Chris wondered again whether she had been the person to alert her father of their leaving. At first he had considered such an act hostile. Now that he thought about it, maybe it was *she* who had saved their lives.

"Hi!" She greeted them with a smile. "Father said I'd find you here. He asked me to tell you it will soon be your turn to eat and rest. There's a sleeping center inside the talonium plant."

"You mean everyone around here takes turns sleeping?" Chris asked, smiling back.

"Of course. That way, the activity never has to shut down. Gat will see that you have food and take you to the sleeping quarters when he returns."

Steve spoke up. "Gat never stops working, does he?"

Kaali chuckled. "Good old Gat. We call him 'Gat of all jobs.' He doesn't have to work this way, you know. Gat is an engineer, a governor on his planet Felson, and a member of the Intergalactic Council that runs these way stations."

"A governor!" Chris exclaimed. "That hairy little guy?"

Kaali frowned. "What's wrong with the way he looks?"

Chris shrugged. "Nothing, I guess, if you like chimpanzees."

Kaali's voice was sharp. "He's a lot more intelligent than you Earthlings! Just because the environment of Felson is more rugged than Earth's and has influenced the appearance of its inhabitants, that doesn't mean the people haven't progressed. It's *their* knowledge of underground living and *their* technology that helped develop this way station."

"If Gat's technology is so advanced," Chris said, "how come he goes along with such old-fashioned methods of mining?"

"Because your Earth scientists have set up probes to monitor the vibrations within the moon. If we use our latest mining equipment, its vibrations would help your people locate our spaceport right away. This 'old-fashioned method,' as you call it, gives off only slight, irregular vibrations." She grinned. "Your scientists think they are monitoring moonquakes."

Gat approached, scowling. "Ore is piling up in there, Earthlings. Stop chattering and get back to work."

The boys trundled the hopper into the tunnel and started its reloading.

Gat called a halt at last, and wearily Chris and Steve trudged after him toward the sleeping quarters. They entered a small room where air vents sucked the ore particles from their clothing. They passed through what looked to Chris like a shower. No water came from the fixture, however, only a strange prickling sensation. Gat ordered Chris to turn around in it. Chris watched in amazement as the dirt and grime disappeared from his hands and arms. His face and hair felt clean too. He had the sensation of having taken a shower.

The sleeping center was a large room sectioned off into alcoves. In each alcove, a soft pad appeared to be suspended a few feet from the floor by an unseen force. Gat assigned each boy to an alcove, handed them several food bars, and left.

Chris sank onto the soft bed and closed his eyes. He was too tired to eat. What a lot had happened in the last sixteen hours! The accident of Steve falling into the rille; the moving tunnel; the spaceport with Monaal, Gat, and Kaali; the piloteer; the attempted escape; and now, the talonium mine. There was no possible chance of escaping from *this* place. The only way they could hope to leave was to prove their trustworthiness to Gat and Monaal.

Chris had to admit he hadn't made a very good start. If he tried harder, though, maybe he could gain Gat's and Monaal's confidence. Come to think of it, it wasn't a matter of *maybe*—he *had* to! With a sigh, he fell asleep.

The next day passed in the same monotonous work. Gat came around periodically to check on them. He seemed less and less offensive to Chris. There were moments when Chris found himself regarding Gat almost as though he were another human being.

The morning of the third day, after a breakfast of space bars, Chris followed Gat and Steve to the mine. As he waited for the hopper to fill, Chris watched Gat adjusting a drill for a Throalian. It wasn't a bit difficult anymore to think of Gat as an engineer, a governor on his planet, and a member of the Intergalactic Council. Now that Chris thought of it, Gat didn't look like an animal at all—just a very hairy person. True, Gat was gruff and wasted no words, but he was far more intelligent than a lot of human beings Chris knew.

He wished he knew Gat better. Did he have a family? Why was he working here on the way station? And why was he working so hard? Chris discussed this with Steve as they dumped ore on the conveyor belt.

Steve glanced back into the tunnel. "I guess he *likes* to work, that's all. Some people are that way—workaholics."

"Yes, I know. My granddad—"

Chris was interrupted by a sudden rumble from the tunnel. The floor under them shook. Someone cried out. It sounded like Gat.

Chris and Steve ran into the tunnel. They were met by a dust cloud full of Throalians racing out.

"Cave-in!" one of them shouted as he passed.

"Where's Gat?" Chris asked.

"Back there." A Throalian pointed. "Under the rocks!"

"Come on!" Chris shouted to Steve. "We've got to get him out!"

CHAPTER 7

A Traitor Aboard?

Steve hesitated at the mouth of the tunnel. "It isn't safe in there, Chris. What if the mine caves in more?"

"We'll have to take that chance," Chris said, waving the dust aside. He loped into the tunnel.

In the dim light, he could see one of Gat's arms extending from under a pile of rubble. He knelt down and began pawing the rocks away.

Steve joined him. Together they uncovered Gat's still form.

There was a low moan from the furry chest. Chris held Gat's shaggy head in his lap. "Quick, Steve, go for help!"

Steve dashed off.

Gat opened his green eyes and looked up at Chris. "What happened?"

"A cave-in. Don't worry. We've dug you out."

"You Earthlings?"

"Sure. Steve's gone for help."

Gat started to rise.

"No, don't move. We have to be sure there are no broken bones."

Gat smiled faintly. "No need to worry about that. I have no bones."

"No bones!"

Gat brushed the rock dust from his chest. "Beneath this fur is a sort of carapace, or bonelike shell, such as your turtles or armadillos have. It's not easily crushed."

"Wow!" Chris exclaimed. "I didn't know people could be built like that."

Gat looked at Chris. "On my planet, Felson, our evolution was slow. It took a long time to develop a physical form that could withstand the environmental pressures." He rose unsteadily to his feet. Chris helped him.

"You'd better rest, Mr. Gat. Even though you've got a solid shell inside, an accident like this can jolt you. Let me help you to the sleeping quarters."

Gat smiled as he leaned on Chris's arm. "Your concern for me is unexpected. What has changed your attitude?"

"Attitude?" Chris felt uncomfortable.

"I've been aware of your opinion of me."

Chris's face flushed. "You mean you've been reading my thoughts?"

"Let us say, your actions."

Chris felt a wave of shame flood over him. What must it have felt like to Gat to realize the low opinion this Earthling held of him? "I—I—Listen, Mr. Gat, I might as well tell you. I'd never seen a being like you until I came here. I thought that only humanoids who looked like *me* were real persons, intelligent enough to develop or understand technology. Now I know better. You're a real person, and one that's a lot smarter than I'll ever be."

Gat smiled. "I think it's time to see Monaal."

Steve, with Throalian helpers, arrived at the tunnel entrance as Chris and Gat were coming out.

Gat waved the helpers aside. "I'm fine now. No need of anyone's assistance." He turned to Steve. "Come. We are going to Monaal." His step was steady.

Through the talonium plant, the tube shuttle, and the hallway, the boys followed Gat to Monaal's office.

Monaal looked questioningly at Gat.

Gat waved his hairy arms at the boys. "Today these Earthlings rescued me from a cave-in. They have proven themselves. I return them to you."

"Fine!" Monaal sounded pleased. "I am grateful to you two for saving my trusted associate here."

"We were glad to help," Chris said. "Now may we leave, sir?"

Monaal looked pensive. "My requirement was that you prove yourselves trustworthy. Rescuing Gat is commendable. I still question your trustworthiness."

"But, Mr. Monaal!" Chris said. "We did everything at the talonium mine Gat asked us to do. Doesn't that prove we're trustworthy?"

"To a degree, yes. However, I have no proof of your *commitment* to this virtue." He pressed a button on his desk. "Tell Brill I'd like to see him."

In a few moments, a willowy being over two meters tall entered the room. His round, protruding eyes, darting from side to side, filled with alarm at sight of the boys.

"Don't be concerned, Brill," Monaal said, nodding toward the boys. "These Earthlings are here by accident. They wish to return to the moon's surface. I need further proof that they can be trusted to keep our way station a secret. Until then, they are to work for you."

Chris, gazing up at the slender giant with the shifty eyes, felt almost as small as Monaal. Brill had shoulder-length blond hair and, like the rest, wore blue coveralls with a red collar and belt. A gismo hung from his neck.

Brill hesitated. "But the work I need done—can they handle it?"

Monaal smiled. "Try them and see."

Brill shrugged and motioned the boys to follow him. Chris had the impression Brill didn't want them around. They entered the long passageway, then the elevator. Chris was sure he knew where they were going as the elevator rose. They entered Hangar One. He was right. He glanced quickly toward the hangar door. Yes, their moon-trike was standing right where they had left it. Steve saw it, too, and grinned at Chris.

Brill led the boys up a ladder and into a circular spaceship. It was roomy inside. In the center was a long metal tube. Around the perimeter of the ship were batteries of consoles with fixed seats in front of them. The floor consisted of metal plates. At one side, these plates were being removed.

The giant handed Chris and Steve each a tool that looked much like a pancake turner with a switch on the handle. "This tool," Brill said in a grating voice, "will release the plates, which are fused by heat. Place it flat over a seam like this. Flip the switch in the handle and leave the tool on the metal till the plate turns red." The metal turned from pink to red. "Now, remove the tool and pry the plate loose with this wedge." He picked up a pry bar and slipped it between the plates. A few shoves and the plates separated. "Be careful," he said. "Don't burn yourselves."

He watched as Chris and Steve followed his directions. Satisfied that they knew what to do, Brill started for a console where wires protruded. "So," Brill said as he studied the wires, "you are from Earth. Quite underdeveloped, I understand."

"Not at all," Chris said. "We have some satellite cities orbiting the planet and some colonies here on the moon. I wouldn't say that was underdeveloped."

Brill attached two wires. "Perhaps not in *your* eyes. But compared to Gamadrome, the planet I come from, you Earthlings are still far from knowing very much."

Steve pried at a plate. "Just what do *you* know that we don't?"

"To answer that question would be like explaining the theory of intergalactic travel to a vegetable."

Chris bristled. "We're not exactly vegetables, Mr. Brill."

"Maybe not," Brill said, chuckling. "Still, you Earthlings have a long way to go before you're ready to mingle with the Gamadromes." He tested a switch. "In fact, even others in this way station could profit from the advancements known on my planet."

Chris looked up. "I thought Monaal said members of the Intergalactic Federation regarded one another as equals."

"They do, in certain ways, but some of us are more equal than others." Brill shrugged and fell silent.

Another giant stuck his head in the doorway. "Brill! Come quickly!"

Brill hastened to his comrade.

"It's almost ready," the stranger said.

"Hush, Dep!" Brill silenced his friend, motioning toward the boys with his eyes.

Dep whispered something to Brill, and the two clambered down the ladder.

Steve glanced around. "What was all *that* about?"

"How should I know? I couldn't hear them." Chris pried at a loose plate. "I don't like this Brill character, do you?"

Steve shook his head. "He's about as conceited as he is tall."

"Yeah! And did you notice those shifty eyes? I wouldn't trust him across the street."

Steve laughed. "Look who's talking about trust!"

"Listen, Steve, I know I made a mistake trying to escape. That's over and done with. It's going to be hard, working with this Gamadrome, Brill, but we've got to earn Monaal's confidence if we expect to get out of here."

"Sure, I read you." Steve gazed out the door of the spacecraft. "But it would be a lot easier if our moontrike wasn't sitting out there all ready to leave through the tunnel."

Chris sat back on his heels. "Don't try anything, Steve. Those beings probably have eyes and ears in the backs of their heads. Another goofed-up escape attempt and we'll *never* be able to leave."

"You're right. Besides, our life-support suits are down there in the lockers." Steve sighed. "One thing's for sure. We're going to know a lot more about the *inside* of the moon than we do about the outside when we get back."

"If we get back!"

The boys had removed a number of plates before Brill returned. He began attaching more wires on the console. Dep, however, kept sidling in and whispering to Brill. Chris noticed Brill glance nervously at them, as though he wished they weren't around. Something mysterious was going on. Chris wished he knew what it was. Why were plates being removed?

Dep stuck his head in the doorway at last and whispered hoarsely, "They're here! Come on!"

Brill left his work and hurried down the ladder. Chris could hear excited voices below. The mystery was too much for him. He had to know what was going on. He signaled to Steve, and they crept closer to the doorway.

"They are ready," one voice said.22222222222

"But it wouldn't be safe to take the complex now," another protested.

"When is it *ever* safe?" It was Brill's voice. "If we Gamadromes are to succeed in this undertaking, we must act within the hour. Take your posts. When I give the signal, we'll move in."

Puzzled, the boys looked at each other. Then Chris's eyes widened. "Steve! Brill and those Gamadromes are planning to take over the way station!"

"Why would they want to do that?"

"Because they think they're superior to everyone, that's why! Quick! We've got to warn Monaal!"

CHAPTER 8

Another Chance

Chris and Steve watched Brill and the Gamadromes hurry away. Quickly the two boys scrambled down the ladder and scooted to the alleyway. They kept glancing behind to see if Brill was following them.

They reached the elevator and descended to the floor where Chris remembered Monaal had his office. They ran down the hall and knocked urgently on his door.

"Come in," Monaal called.

Chris and Steve rushed inside. Monaal, with his back to them, was standing in front of the transparent map, moving the magnetic disks about. "What can I do for you?" He turned and looked with surprise at the panting boys.

"Mr. Monaal," Chris said, "I'm sorry to bother you, but we just found out your way station is in trouble."

"Trouble? What kind of trouble?"

Steve spoke. "It's Brill—"

"Yes," Chris said. "He and a bunch of Gamadromes are planning to take over the way station."

Monaal looked puzzled. "Take over the way station? That's impossible! The Gamadromes wouldn't do a thing like that."

"But they are," Chris assured him. "We overheard them planning the whole operation just a minute ago."

Monaal motioned for the boys to sit down in front of his desk. "Now, tell me exactly what you heard."

Chris described the conversation he and Steve had overheard in the spacecraft. "You've got to act quickly to stop them, Mr. Monaal," Chris said. "Brill told them they would move within the hour."

Monaal shook his head. "This can't happen in the Intergalactic Federation. We settled all our differences centuries ago. Brill isn't that kind of person."

"But he is," Chris said. "He thinks he and all the Gamadromes are a lot smarter than the others here in the way station. He told us so himself."

"Yes," Steve said. "He thinks we Earthlings are vegetables. Boy, is he wrong!"

Monaal reached across his desk. "I will call Brill in at once to explain this."

Chris held out a protesting hand. "No, don't call him. He'll deny the whole thing. We wanted you to know his plot so you could alert the other beings in the way station to be on guard."

"There's no need for such an alert. I'm sure Brill is to be trusted."

Chris leaned forward. "Look, Mr. Monaal, why don't you come to the hangar with us and check this out for yourself?"

"A good idea!" Monaal rose and started for the door.

"Aren't you going to take a weapon of some kind?" Chris asked.

Monaal shook his head. "We have no need for weapons here. I trust Brill." He led the way out of the room.

"Brother!" Steve muttered. "I'd feel better if he had a ray gun or something."

The three entered the hangar as Brill emerged from the spacecraft. *"There* you are," he said as he saw the boys with Monaal. "I've been looking for you two. Those plates must be removed at once."

Monaal, to Chris's surprise, marched up to Brill and said, "What is this I hear about you and your fellow Gamadromes taking over the way station?"

"Taking over the way station!" Brill looked startled, then threw back his head and laughed.

Monaal looked at the boys. "These two claim you are planning to take the complex, to move in when you give your Gamadromes the signal."

Brill looked first at the boys, then at Monaal.

"Do you deny that you said this?" Monaal demanded.

"Of course, I don't deny it!" Brill exclaimed. "They are right."

Chris looked at Steve in astonishment.

"But the 'complex' I was talking about is not the way station; it's that shipment of dangerous complex metals—talonium mixed with zycon—scheduled to go to Gamadrome today. You yourself know their elements become unstable if allowed to mingle when not under pressure. We have to move them as quickly as possible."

Monaal's face relaxed. His eyes twinkled as he looked at the boys. "You see? Your fears were unfounded. Brill is right. I had forgotten that shipment was due to leave today. It requires both care and speed."

Chris lowered his eyes. He felt uncomfortable. "I'm sorry we bothered you, Mr. Monaal. We didn't know Brill was talking about a shipment of dangerous stuff."

Monaal patted Chris's arm. "I understand, and I'm pleased that in your mistaken belief, your concern for the way station prompted you to report to me. Your trustworthiness is making progress." He turned and left.

Brill pointed to the ladder. "Back to work, Earthlings. This shipment must leave soon." He smiled. "And keep those imaginations of yours toned down."

Chris and Steve hurried up the ladder. Chris was relieved that Brill didn't hold a grudge against them. If it had been their Scoutmaster, Mr. Bryant, he would have lectured them on not jumping to conclusions, on not crying "wolf" when there was no need for it. Perhaps Monaal was right. No hostility existed among members of the Intergalactic Federation. Trust had taken its place. What a great feeling it must be to trust everyone! Chris was certainly willing to try it with Brill.

Just as the boys finished removing the floor plates of the spacecraft and were climbing down the ladder, some Gamadromes entered the hangar. They were carrying small black boxes, which they carefully lifted into the spacecraft and then lowered into the special new hold under the floor, where the plates had been removed.

The crew boarded, and lights began to flash around the craft's perimeter. Steve hurried to get the moontrike out of the way of the hangar door.

Brill came over, pulling on space gloves. He grinned down at Chris and Steve. "Too bad you Earthlings can't accompany me to Gamadrome and see what you're missing."

"Yeah," Steve said. "I'd like to see what we 'vegetables' don't know."

Brill chuckled. "I never said you Earthlings were vegetables. I used that expression as a comparison of progress between two cultures. I hope there are no hard feelings."

Chris shook his head slowly. "No hard feelings, Mr. Brill."

The boys watched Brill climb into the spacecraft. The hangar doors slid into the walls, and the craft rolled onto the tunnel floor. It moved slowly down the tunnel as the doors closed again.

"Hey," Steve said, "did you see how they activated the door and tunnel floor?"

"No," Chris said, "and I don't want to know."

"Why not?"

"Can't you figure that out?"

Steve put his hands on his hips. "No, I can't. What's wrong with you, Chris? This is our chance to get out of here. *I* saw how they opened the door and activated the tunnel floor." He pointed. "It's done by that bar in the floor. Our moontrike is ready, and no one's around. All we have to do is slip down to the locker, grab our life-support suits, and we're home free!"

Chris started for the door leading to the alleyway. "Go ahead and leave. I'm staying."

"What's with you, Chris? This is it! There's no way our escape can fail this time."

Chris opened the door and turned. "Sure, Steve, maybe so. But something else mustn't fail, either—*trusting* people."

CHAPTER 9

Cyclo

Chris headed for the elevator. Steve trailed him. "Where are you going?" Steve asked as the elevator descended.

"Back to Monaal. If he says it's okay for us to leave, I'll leave."

Steve grinned. "Hey, now you're talking. He's bound to let us go. We've done everything he asked us to do. We've been trustworthy." Chris glanced at Steve and raised his eyebrows.

Steve shrugged and waved a hand. "That last idea of mine—just a suggestion. Forget it."

They found Monaal with his daughter. Monaal greeted the boys with a smile. "I've been expecting you," he said. "Brill informed me from his craft, as he left, that you performed your tasks well, and I see you resisted the temptation to leave after him."

Chris looked earnestly at Monaal. "Then may we leave now, please?"

Monaal turned to his daughter. "I think they've proven they can keep the secret of this way station to themselves, don't you, Kaali?"

"Of course, they can," Kaali said, smiling.

Chris's face grew solemn. "What about my Granddad Jerry? Can't I tell even him that I met you and that all these things happened to Steve and me?"

Monaal laid a hand on Chris's arm. "Of course, you may tell Jerry, but—"

Chris nodded. "I know—nobody else. I promise."

"That goes for me too," Steve said.

"Then, yes, you may go now," Monaal said.

"Gee, thanks, Mr. Monaal!" Chris's voice was happy.

"Yes, sir! Thank you!" Steve reached for Monaal's hand and pumped it up and down.

Monaal waved them to the door. "Go. Put on your life-support suits."

Chris hesitated at the door. "There's one thing, though. After we leave the tunnel, how do we get out of the rille? Its sides are too steep to climb with our moontrike."

"There's an easy trail to the right of the tunnel entrance," Kaali said. "I used to explore out there, before your moon colonies were established." She looked at her father. "Why don't I put on a space suit and show them where it is?"

"Good idea," Monaal said. "When you boys are suited up, come back here. Kaali will go with you."

The boys raced down the hall to the locker room and pulled on their life-support suits. With their headgear tucked under their arms, they returned to Monaal's office. In her silver-colored space suit, Kaali was waiting for them. They started for the elevator.

Kaali sighed. "I'm sorry you're leaving so soon. I wanted to ask you lots of questions about Earth and your satellite city."

"I wanted to ask you about Throal, too," Chris said, "but your dad kept us pretty busy."

"Yes, I know. He's really concerned about the secrecy of this way station. You see, there are others who are trying to join the

Intergalactic Federation, but are not ready yet. They're still too war-like, and they think they can force themselves in—like Cyclo."

"Cyclo? Where is that?" Chris asked.

"It's not a place; it's a person. Cyclo rules the planet Jovan in the galaxy of Woss."

"Jovan?" Steve said. "I've heard that name before. Gat told us not to hook our piloteer onto any Jovan craft—that this way station was off limits to them."

Kaali nodded. "It certainly is. Jovan has a very strange mixture of people. How such a warlike culture developed its knowledge of space, we'll never know. My father's had several run-ins with Cyclo. Father refuses to let Jovan join the Federation."

The elevator took them to the upper level, where they passed through the alleyway and into Hangar One. They laid their headgear aside while they readied the moontrike. Before they were through, however, the hangar door began to slide open. Chris could see the glint of light on a metallic surface. A small one-person spacecraft was approaching.

The three moved back to allow the craft to enter. Mist eddied about its bottom as three legs glided downward from the ship. The fourth leg stuck halfway down as the craft settled on the hangar floor. The hangar door closed behind it.

Chris heard Kaali gasp and glanced around at her.

She was pointing at the craft. "Look!"

Chris looked upward at the emblem on the bottom of the ship. It was an unmistakable *J* with a spear through it, the emblem of Jovan!

Kaali swallowed. "How could anyone have found this entrance? It's hardly ever used."

Chris shook his head. "I don't know, unless they saw Brill leave."

"That must have been it," Kaali said. "Quick! We've got to tell Father!" She started for the door.

A figure emerged from the side of the craft. "Stay where you are!" he barked in a deep voice. Chris watched the being descend by a light shaft to the hangar floor. He was taller than Chris and wore a silver suit. From a small black box in front of him blinked a blue light. The figure turned to face them, and Chris gasped in surprise. The being had one large penetrating eye in the center of his forehead.

His nose consisted of two slits, and his mouth a straight line. The corners of his mouth turned up slightly. It was not a pleasant smile.

"Aren't you going to welcome me, Kaali?" the being asked.

Kaali gulped and nervously clasped the gismo at her neck. "You are *not* welcome, Cyclo, and you know it!" She drew close to Chris and Steve.

"So this is Cyclo!" Chris whispered.

Cyclo circled them. "I'm sure your father will change his mind when he hears my plan." He stared at the boys. "Who are these beings?"

"They are Earthlings," Kaali answered.

"Earthlings, eh? What are *they* doing here? Earth does not belong to the Federation."

Chris looked into the penetrating eye of Cyclo. "We were just leaving, sir."

"So! Earth is being allowed the courtesies of the Federation, and Jovan is not! Earth! That puny planet that is light-years behind Jovan."

"Oh, that's not it at all, sir," Chris said. "Steve and I just wandered in here by accident and—"

Cyclo waved his hands impatiently. "I have no time for explanations. You are, unfortunately, in the way, and I shall have to dispose of you." He motioned them toward his craft.

Chris held back. Cyclo touched the black box, and a beam of blue light shot out. Chris felt a painful tingling in his left arm where the beam hit. He moved with the others toward the spacecraft.

Chris hesitated again when he reached the shaft of light. Cyclo shoved him roughly into it, and he found himself being drawn upward into the craft. Kaali and Steve followed, with Cyclo right behind. The craft was much smaller than Brill's and designed for one person to operate. Windows, invisible from the outside, circled the perimeter of the ship.

Kaali stood defiantly in front of Cyclo. "If you think you can intimidate my father, you're mistaken."

Cyclo shoved the three to the far side of the craft and pointed the black box at them threateningly.

"Stay there," he ordered, then smiled at Kaali. "I have no need to intimidate Monaal." He sat down in the swivel chair in front of a battery of switches and fights. Cyclo pressed a button. The craft door closed. He reached for a switch. "This is Cyclo from the planet Jovan in the galaxy of Woss, calling Monaal in way station, natural satellite planet three, Kyclos galaxy. I have a message for you."

There was a sputtering of static, then Monaal's crisp voice. "What do you want, Cyclo?"

"You know what I want—membership for Jovan in the Intergalactic Federation."

"That is the message?" Monaal sounded impatient. "I've heard it before. The answer is negative!"

"Oh, but I think you will reconsider, now that I have Kaali, your daughter." Cyclo's voice was hard. "Her safety—for Jovan's membership in the Federation."

"That's blackmail!" Chris whispered to Steve.

Monaal was silent for a moment. "Where do you have her?"

Kaali rushed forward, suddenly shouting, "I'm in Cyclo's spacecraft with Chris and Steve. We're in—" but she got no further.

Cyclo rose quickly, put his hand over her mouth, and pushed her roughly back against the boys. He pointed the black box at her menacingly, then turned to the switchboard. "Let us just say, she's with me and will be released when you agree to my request." He snapped off the communication switch, reached into a compartment, and drew out a length of cord.

He ordered the three to a shaft in the center of the craft. Deftly he tied their hands behind them, forced them to sit with their backs to the shaft, then wrapped the cord around all of them.

"Now you are safe while I check my ship's landing gear." He leaned over and patted Kaali on the head. "Your father is a reasonable man. We'll be hearing from him soon." Cyclo picked up a toolbox, strode to the door of the craft, and left by the beam of light.

Steve turned toward Chris. "How do we get into messes like this?"

Chris shrugged. "We're just lucky, I guess."

CHAPTER 10

A Throalian Gift

Kaali leaned forward, twisting her wrists. "That's not funny, Chris. We're in real trouble. What are we going to do?"

Chris wriggled his wrists behind him. "Don't worry, Kaali. Your father will probably send over a whole gang of Throalians. *They'll* take care of Cyclo."

Kaali frowned. "Father doesn't know we're inside his way station. That's what I was trying to tell him before Cyclo pushed me away."

"Look," Steve said. "The guard in the alleyway is bound to check out the hangar. Once he sees this craft's emblem, he'll alert Monaal."

"Didn't you notice? The guard isn't there anymore. He was only guarding Brill's ship." Kaali sighed as she strained at the cords. "No one ever comes up here. This hangar has been used only rarely since your moon colonies were established. Brill had to keep his craft below the rille's edge until he was out of range of your detectors before he could take off for space."

Chris leaned from side to side as he worked at his bound wrists. "So why was Brill in here and not in the main hangar?"

"His ship was to be loaded with dangerous materials under pressure. It was safer in here away from the other craft."

"Hey, look at this!" Chris exclaimed, holding one hand in front of him. "I worked loose." He pulled the cords from his wrists. "Hold still, you two, and I'll free you." He twisted around, untied the cord that bound them together against the shaft, then untied Kaali's and Steve's hands.

Steve stood up and rubbed his wrists. "What do we do now? Cyclo could come back here any minute." He listened intently. "What's all that banging going on underneath us?"

Kaali cocked her head. "He's working on that landing leg that's stuck."

Chris tiptoed to the console. He beckoned to Kaali. "Have you ever flown one of these craft before?"

She nodded. "We have some like it on Throal."

"Then which of these switches retracts the landing legs?"

She peered at the switchboard for a second before pointing. "It's this one right here."

"You're sure?"

"Yes." She looked in alarm as Chris reached for the switch. "What are you going to do?"

"I'm going to surprise Cyclo," Chris said. "Hang on, everyone." He threw the switch suddenly, and the craft plummeted to the hangar floor with a loud clank. There was an equally loud yell from underneath.

The sudden descent caused a few moments of airborne confusion. Chris and Kaali hung on to the swivel chair beside the switchboard. Steve, unaware of Chris's action, rose in the air, thumping his head on the craft's ceiling. He landed on his hands and knees on the floor.

"What happened?" he asked.

Chris started for the door. "From the yelling out there, I'd say we've caught Cyclo. Come on. Let's get out of here."

They scrambled to the door and jumped out. Cyclo lay pinned to the floor under the landing gear he had been repairing. Chris could see that he was not badly hurt. The full weight of the craft had missed him. He lay on his back like an overturned beetle, waving his arms and legs as he tried to free himself.

"Sorry, Cyclo," Chris said. "Blackmail won't work. Jovan, just like Earth, has to *earn* a place in the Intergalactic Federation." He followed Steve and Kaali as they headed for the alleyway.

Kaali was greeted with happy shouts as she neared Monaal's office. Throalians crowded around his door. Monaal ran out to meet her, followed closely by Gat. Chris and Steve stood back as father and daughter hugged each other.

Monaal beckoned to the boys. Inside his office, he and Gat beamed at them as Kaali told of Chris's clever maneuver.

"What will happen to Cyclo?" Chris asked.

"We will free him and send him back to Jovan in his craft," Monaal said.

Steve frowned. "What if he brings back others from Jovan and tries to take this way station?"

"He's not likely to," Monaal answered. "Cyclo works alone, and he's a clever being. He'll learn in time that meeting our Federation's standards is easier than trying to get around them. But come. You two should be on your way. When did you say you had to be back at your moonport?"

Chris struck his forehead with his hand. "I'd forgotten all about that! We have to be back today by 6:00 p.m." He glanced at his watch. "Oh, no, it's almost that time now! We'll never make it."

Monaal hurried to his desk and pushed a button on his intercom. "Bring a Z-wing to Hangar One at once."

Steve looked quizzically at Chris, who shrugged.

Kaali saw their reaction and smiled. "Don't worry. A Z-wing will get you back faster than you can recite your own alphabet." Monaal, Kaali, and Gat accompanied the boys to Hangar One.

Throalians were already there helping Cyclo out from under his spacecraft. The blue light he wore in front of him was out. Chris watched him limp into his ship and steer it out through the hangar door.

Their headgear was lying near the moon-trike where they had left it earlier. A Throalian brought a package to Monaal.

Monaal opened it. "Here is our Z-wing," he said, unfolding a fragile-looking pair of wings, each a meter long. A small box with two levers joined them in the center.

Monaal attached the Z-wing to the moon-trike handlebars and pressed a button. The wings glowed yellow. He pointed at the levers. "This one to the left will lift your moontrike or lower it. The lever on the right will carry it forward or backward. When you arrive at your destination, press this button on the bottom." He smiled. "You'll be back with your Scout troop in no time."

The boys put on their headgear.

Monaal reached into a pocket and drew out a small package. "I have something here for Jerry. You are fortunate to have such a talented grandfather, Chris, and he such a fine grandson. Please give this to him and tell him Monaal sends greetings."

"Thanks. I sure will." Chris took the package and put it in his inside shirt pocket.

As Monaal and Gat shook the boys' hands, Monaal said, "I expect to see both of you again. Perhaps, in the years ahead, you'll become two of Earth's envoys to our Intergalactic Federation."

Kaali shook their hands, too, and smiled. "I'd like that."

The boys fastened their headgear, got onto their moontrike, and rolled it over the floor bar that activated the hangar door. They waved to Monaal, Kaali, and Gat as they entered the tunnel with its moving floor.

At the tunnel's entrance, Steve pressed the left lever on the Z-wing, and the trike rose rapidly to the rille's rim. Once out of the rille, he lifted the trike a few centimeters above the ground and applied the right lever. The trike skimmed like a hovercraft over the moonscape.

"Wow! This is great!" he exclaimed over the intercom. "It even beats hill-climbing."

In minutes, they were back at the moon-port. At its entrance, Steve stopped and climbed off. "Wowie! I'm keeping this Z-wing!"

Chris reached over and pressed the button underneath as Monaal had instructed them to do.

Both boys watched in horror as the Z-wing shriveled into a twisted mass, then wisped away like blown ashes.

"What did you have to do that for?" Steve said.

"How was I to know it would self-destruct!" Chris answered. "I guess Monaal thought this was just one more thing we Earthlings—"

"Weren't ready for yet!" the two Scouts chorused together.

Inside the moonport, Mr. Bryant ran toward them with joy that soon turned to anger. Thank heavens they were safe! Where had they been? His mustache twitched excitedly as the boys climbed out of their life-support suits. Did they realize everybody had been looking for them? The troop was almost ready to leave without them. He was really disappointed in their behavior. Until they could prove they understood what being "trustworthy" meant, there'd be no more trips for them. He'd see to that!

Chris and Steve boarded the moon shuttle with the rest of the Scouts and strapped themselves into their seats. Mr. Bryant's remarks still swirled about them like angry bees.

Chris sighed, looked out the window, and said nothing. He couldn't talk. Trustworthiness? He knew its meaning all right—better than anybody here, outside of Steve, of course. His eyes met Steve's. Steve wasn't talking either. Nothing Mr. Bryant or anyone else could do would make them tell what had happened to them in the last three days. Monaal needn't worry.

Chris leaned back and listened to the pilot and copilot discussing a streak of light they had seen earlier snaking through a rille. Was it Brill's departure? Chris wondered.

Suddenly he sat up and looked at Steve. "Hey, aren't those the same pilots who brought us here?"

"Sure are," Steve said. "Remember? They talked in Swedish like that all the time."

Chris reached into his breast pocket and fingered the package Monaal had given him for his granddad. He leaned back and smiled. *That wasn't Swedish he heard just now!* Oh, wow! Was Granddad Jerry going to be happy to get *this* gift!

A MESSAGE FROM MONAAL

To David.

CHAPTER 1

A Mysterious Gift

From the small windows of Moon Shuttle 720, Satellite City Alpha looked to Chris Cole like a gigantic wheel slowly rotating in space. Its spokes were attached to a thick hub, below which extended a long slender rod. Chris leaned back in the shuttle seat and surveyed the reflector poised above the city like a giant coin with a hole in the middle. He could see it was slanted to catch the sun's rays and reflect them into the continuous windows that lined the inner wall of the wheel. He was glad to be getting home before the mirror was tilted to simulate night in Alpha City. In the distance the planet Earth looked just like a cloudy blue marble.

Chris leaned close to his friend Steve Gregg, sitting next to him. "I'll bet our Scoutmaster is plenty glad to get home."

"Yeah," Steve said. "Our three-day trip to the moon hasn't ex- actly been a picnic for him."

Chris grinned. "Or for you and me either."

Steve spread his hands. "Why do we always get into trouble?"

Chris shrugged and glanced back at Mr. Bryant, the Scoutmaster, who was running a finger nervously around his collar. "I wouldn't call what happened to you and me trouble. It was fantastic—finding that intergalactic way station inside the moon and meeting that neat leader Monaal and the other beings from outer space."

"Sure," Steve said. "But I meant getting into trouble with Bryant. There's no way we can tell him what really happened when we got separated from the rest of the troop—no way."

Chris nodded. "I don't care if I get kicked out of the troop. I'll never tell anyone about Monaal's secret way station."

"Me neither." Steve glanced around. "I wonder how many meteors the guys collected up on the moon. That's what we were supposed to go after in the first place, wasn't it?"

"Yes, and picking up the pieces of that historic lunar rover that the meteors clobbered." Chris frowned. "I guess we'll learn soon enough—if Bryant lets us stay in the troop."

Mr. Bryant cleared his throat and said loudly, "Okay, fellows, we're nearing the docking bay. I don't want any of you to leave the spaceport until your parents or other relatives arrive to take you home. Is that clear?"

Chris sighed. "Oh, man! Bryant's really going to bend our folks' ears about our lack of cooperation and all that stuff!"

"He sure is," Steve said. "What are we going to do?"

"We're not going to talk, that's what! If we don't give them an argument, they may think we're sorry and get off our backs."

The moon shuttle nosed up to the docking bay like a baby whale nuzzling its mother. The extended accordion chute fastened to the shuttle with a soft thud. The air locks hissed a moment. Then the shuttle door slid open.

In the waiting room stood families, waving and grinning as the Scouts piled out. Steve found and greeted his dad, who whisked him off to their waiting electric car. Chris looked about for his parents. They weren't there. Then he caught sight of red hair sprinkled lightly with gray. It was his Grandfather Jerry!

Chris hurried forward. "Hi, Jerry!" he called as the athletic man of eighty, who looked more like forty, strode toward him and gave him a bear hug.

Jerry stepped back. "Sorry your dad and mom couldn't make it, Chris. They had a consulting job of some kind in Beta City. You're staying with your grandmother and me until they get back."

"Great!" Chris said.

"How was the trip?" Jerry asked. But before Chris could answer, Mr. Bryant hurried over.

"Pardon me, sir, but are you related to Chris?" the Scoutmaster asked.

Chris sensed trouble and spoke up quickly. "Yes, he's my grandfather, Jerry Cole. Jerry, this is my Scoutmaster, Mr. Bryant." Jerry extended a hand, and Mr. Bryant shook it briefly.

"Jerry?" Mr. Bryant frowned at Chris. "You call your grandfather by his first name?"

"Sure. Why not?" Chris asked.

"Well," Mr. Bryant said, "I'd think you would show more respect for adults."

Chris's grandfather smiled. "Age has nothing to do with it, Mr. Bryant. Chris and I are buddies. Right, Chris?"

"Right!"

"Hhmm," Mr. Bryant said, looking at Chris. "Well, I think your grandfather—ah, Jerry—should know that your behavior on this trip was most unsatisfactory, not becoming a Scout at all!"

Jerry raised his eyebrows. "Is that so?"

Mr. Bryant frowned and continued. "Chris and his friend Steve disappeared the first day we started our retrieval work on the moon, and they didn't turn up until a few minutes before we were due to leave. I'm sure you can understand my concern."

"Indeed I can," Jerry said, glancing at Chris.

Mr. Bryant went on. "Your grandson refuses to discuss where he was or what he did during those three days. I find that quite contrary to the attitude of a good Scout."

Chris studied his feet.

"I hope, sir, that you will impress on Chris the seriousness of his behavior. A Scout must be trustworthy above all else."

Jerry frowned. "You're right, Mr. Bryant. I'll give this problem my attention."

Mr. Bryant nodded his approval and left.

Chris looked up at Jerry. Would his grandfather feel as Mr. Bryant did? Would there be a "what-did-you-do-that-for" accusation? He'd better explain at once.

"You're not going to believe what really happened to Steve and me during those three days," he said quickly. "We couldn't tell Mr. Bryant because we'd promised Monaal we wouldn't."

"Monaal!" Jerry's eyes widened. "You saw Monaal?"

"Yes, and his daughter Kaali too. They're terrific people."

Jerry shook his head in wonder. "I can't believe it! Why, it's been seventy years since I talked to that little spaceman from Throal. He took back the gismo I found—that fantastic language converter I told you about."

"Sure, I know."

"What was Monaal doing on the moon?"

Chris glanced about, then lowered his voice. "I can't tell you here."

Jerry reached down for Chris's spacecase. "Then we'll discuss it later. Come on. Let's get going."

Chris followed Jerry through the sliding doors onto the broad tree-lined sidewalk that led to the street. Jerry's electric runabout stood at the curb. They stowed Chris's gear in back, then climbed into the contoured seats.

Jerry maneuvered the runabout over the grooved track in the right-hand lane. He lowered the contact bar, and they sped away, the car controlled by the electric current in the roadbed.

Jerry rotated his seat to face Chris. "So you met Monaal! Tell me all about it."

"First of all," Chris said, "what I'm about to say is classified information. You're the only person Monaal said I could tell it to. Okay?"

"Okay," Jerry said. "I remember how Monaal wanted his presence kept a secret before."

As the runabout skimmed along the track, Chris told Jerry how the moontrike he and Steve were riding had fallen into a deep rille, or canyon, on the moon. When they'd gone after it, they'd found a tunnel with a moving floor that took them to the interior of the moon. There the intergalactic way station, under Monaal's direction, flourished in the gas-belt tunnels. Chris explained how Monaal wouldn't let them leave until they could prove they were trustworthy enough not to tell anyone about the way station, for even Earth's government knew nothing of its existence.

Chris told, too, of Cyclo, the one-eyed leader of the warlike planet Jovan in the galaxy of Woss, who was trying to force his way into the Intergalactic Federation. Monaal had warned Steve and Chris not to let any spaceship from Jovan enter the station. They could identify such a ship by Jovan's symbol painted underneath—a large J with a spear through it.

Finally Chris described the people from the other galaxies whom he and Steve had met. Although these people were strange in appearance—some completely covered in hair, and others tall and willowy with round protruding eyes—Chris had grown to accept and understand them.

"And you know something?" Chris said. "After I met all those great people and worked with them, I didn't *want* anyone else to know about the way station, except you." He spread his hands. "That's why Steve and I didn't tell Mr. Bryant about where we'd been or what we'd been doing—to prove to Monaal that we could be trustworthy!" He smiled ironically.

Jerry shook his head. "That was quite an adventure, Chris. I can hardly take it all in. But you must understand Mr. Bryant's concern over your disappearance. I think I would have been as upset as he was."

"But we couldn't give away Monaal's secret," Chris protested.

"Of course you couldn't, and I commend you for that. Still, I think you owe Mr. Bryant some explanation for your disappearance and should let him know you'll be more cooperative in the future."

Chris sighed. "I guess so. But I don't know what I can say."

Jerry smiled. "You'll think of something, I'm sure."

He swung his seat around, took charge of the controls, and slowed down the runabout. He guided the car onto a narrow road leading up a short hill to a cantilevered house set among maple trees. The hill was actually an interior slope of the giant toroid, or curved cylinder, that enveloped the space city of Alpha. The atmosphere in the cylinder simulated that of Earth. Small clouds floated high above in the curved interior. The slow rotation of the city kept the gravity the same as on Earth.

Chris climbed out of the runabout, gathered up his gear, and with Jerry rode an elevator to the patio roof garden, where Peg, his grandmother, met him with a hug and a kiss.

"It's good to see you, Chris," she said. "Are you as hungry as ever?"

Chris grinned. "I could sure use a glass of goat's milk and a couple of your great yogurt cookies."

She smiled. "They've been waiting for you." She hurried into the house.

Chris walked to the edge of the garden and looked across at the houses on the opposite slope. Alpha City was seven kilometers from side to side and twenty-two kilometers around.

"Man!" Chris said. "It sure feels good to be home again. That moonscape was creepy! No trees, no houses—just big boulders, craters, rilles, and dust. I hope I don't have to go there very often."

His grandmother returned and handed Chris the refreshments. The communication center beeped, and she ran into the house to answer it.

Jerry smiled. "I'm curious, Chris. How is it that the intergalactic way station has never been detected by Earth's exploration parties? They have seismic probes set up on the moon. And as a member of the United Nations Committee on Space Colonization, I would have heard whether the moon colonies and mining operations had turned up evidence of a way station."

Chris took a long gulp of milk. "Monaal says that because the moon is mostly hollow—filled with those gas tunnels—detection of the way station is difficult." He grinned. "Besides, our scientists think that what they're hearing in their seismic probes are moonquakes."

"How do they enter the station without being seen?"

"On the back side of the moon."

"That figures." Jerry stroked his chin. "I liked that little fellow Monaal. I wonder if he remembers me."

Chris set his glass on a picnic table nearby. "Sure he does. In fact, he sends you his greetings—and this." Chris reached into his shirt pocket and pulled out a small package.

Jerry took it. "What is it?"

Chris's eyes danced. "Go ahead. Open it and see!"

Jerry carefully unwrapped the package. It contained a small metal box. He unsnapped the latch and raised the lid. Inside was a miniature magnetic-card recorder with tiny dials, buttons, and a narrow expandable wristband of silver-colored metal.

Chris's face fell. He'd been sure the gift was a gismo, one of the language converters everyone used at the way station. Gismos converted the vibrations of a person's voice into words that could be understood by a person who didn't know the language being spoken.

On his way home from the moon, Chris had been able to understand the pilots, who were talking in Swedish.

Jerry turned the gift over in his hand. "I've never seen a card recorder this small before." He slipped it onto his wrist and pressed a button on the top.

A high-pitched hum sounded. Then a voice said, *"Greetings, Jerry. This is Monaal of Throal speaking."*

Chris looked at his grandfather. "Do you hear that?"

Jerry waved for quiet.

The voice continued:

"I understand, Jerry, that you have gone far as a designer of Earth's satellite cities. I have also learned that you are a member of Earth's United Nations. Congratulations!

"You occupy a most important position—a position that offers great possibilities for the future of Planet Earth.

"I recall your desire as a boy to see Earth become a member of our Intergalactic Federation. Your planet is now ready for this step. Are you? If so, you can take the lead in achieving it. Your grandson and his friend Steve are, like you, fine examples of Earthlings. I have no doubt that they, too, with your help, will become leaders in the government of your planet.

"My associates and I know it takes great courage, intelligence, and determination to be a responsible leader. We believe you have these qualities, but we must be sure. Therefore, if you truly wish your planet to become a member of the Intergalactic Federation, you must perform three tasks that we have prepared for you. Decode the message inside this instrument and you will learn what the three tasks are.

"This is Monaal of Throal wishing you success."

There was a faint hum, then silence.

Jerry and Chris looked at each other without speaking, momentarily overcome by the importance of Monaal's message.

Finally Jerry said, "Well, that sounds like a pretty tall order. I guess we'd better find out just how tall." Carefully he slipped the recorder from his wrist and turned it over.

Chris peered at the tiny instrument in his grandfather's hand. "It must run on dichips, right?"

"Wrong." Now that the initial shock at Monaal's challenge was easing, Jerry's excitement was growing. He fumbled eagerly with the catches on the back of the recorder. "There's only one thing I know of that can bring Monaal's voice to us." At last the back of the recorder swung open. Jerry let out a low whistle.

Chris grinned. "I knew it! I knew it!"

There, filling the back of the card recorder, was a small rectangle the size of a domino. Tiny knobs extended from either end and a third knob from one side. The upper surface was covered with short brush-like wires, soft and silky as fur. They were fading from cherry red to silver.

Jerry let out a happy sigh. "At last! My very own gismo!"

Chris looked puzzled. "But where is the message?"

CHAPTER 2

The Message

Jerry detached the gismo carefully and turned it over in his hand.

Chris took the tiny card-recorder case and peered inside. A red inch-square plastic card embossed with metal symbols was visible. "There's nothing in here but the card we just heard," Chris said. "Do you suppose Monaal forgot to put the message inside?"

"Not Monaal," Jerry said, still examining the gismo. He looked closely at the sides of the silvery rectangle, tilting it back and forth. "All I can see is a decorative pattern of lines engraved between the side knobs."

"No message?"

"None."

"Crumb!" Chris said. "How could Monaal be so forgetful? If he said there would be a message, there should *be* one!"

"I don't think it's Monaal's fault," Jerry said. "Let's play the card again. Maybe we missed something." He reattached the gismo to the recorder and pressed the start button. The high-pitched voice of Monaal repeated the same message.

Again Jerry opened the recorder and removed the gismo. "It's got to be in here, Chris," he said, frowning as he studied the silvery rectangle. Suddenly he looked up. "Wait a minute! I think I see it!"

"Where?" Chris leaned forward eagerly. "Come!" Jerry hurried inside the house and over to his desk with its built-in computer console. He sat down and switched on the comdat in front of him. Its screen glowed softly. He held up the gismo. "See these lines, Chris— the ones that decorate the sides? They could be coded for a computer. Let's try it out."

"How?"

Jerry reached for a pen attached to the comdat by a spiral cord. He flicked the switch on the side of the pen, and a light glowed at the point. "This scanner pen," he said, "will read the lines on the gismo and feed the information into the terminal. Let's hope the data bank can come up with a translation." He ran the lighted pen point slowly around the gismo.

There was a moment's hesitation. Then green words began to form on the comdat's screen.

Chris leaned over his grandfather's shoulder. "Hey! You're right!"

Together they read:

> On Planet Earth are three messages that fit into this recorder and cite conditions for membership in the Intergalactic Federation. Find these and deliver them, in turn, to your United Nations of Earth. If your government agrees to the conditions set down by the Intergalactic Federation, obtain from the ruling body a written statement to this effect and deliver the document to us at a meeting on the moon. Chris will know where.
>
> The messages are at the following locations
>
> > 1. 29° longitude east; 63° latitude north
> > 2. 72° longitude west; 13° latitude south
> > 3. 78° longitude west; 27° latitude north
>
> *Monaal of Throal*
> Director, Intergalactic Federation

Chris stared at the message on the comdat screen. "How does Monaal know the latitudes and longitudes on Earth?"

"Simple," Jerry answered. "He's studied Earth for a long time. He knew a lot about it even when I was a boy."

"Wow!" Chris sat down beside his grandfather. "This is really a far-out project!"

"You're not kidding, Chris! Farther out than I could have dreamed." Jerry's face grew serious as he looked at his grandson. "It's a huge responsibility. The future of our planet depends on reaching out to other civilizations—becoming a part of the Intergalactic Federation. I'm willing to follow Monaal's orders, but will the United Nations go along with the conditions he sets down?"

Chris shrugged. "How can we know until we find out what those conditions are?"

Jerry smiled. "Good reasoning, Chris. I could use someone like you on this mission. Would you be willing to help me?"

"Willing!" Chris said. "Of course I'm willing! Who wouldn't be?"

"Then copy down those locations." Jerry handed Chris a pad and a pen. Chris copied carefully.

Then Jerry reached over to the console and pushed down a lever. Immediately a hologram of the world globe glowed in front of them. Jerry turned another knob on the console that rotated the image slowly.

"You know," he said, "this means locating on that vast planet three magnetic cards no larger than an inch square. It will be like finding a diode in a black hole."

Chris nodded. "But Monaal and the others wouldn't have asked us to do it if they thought we couldn't. They must have sent their messengers down to Earth in one of those spacecraft I saw at the way station, then planted the messages." He pointed at the paper in his hand. "What I can't figure out is those symbols in front of the locations."

Jerry pressed a series of buttons on the comdat, and the symbols and their interpretations shone beside the globe on the screen. He ran his finger along them as he spoke. "A solid-colored triangle means a mountain. Three dots set in a triangle shape mean ruins of some kind. A line-drawn triangle means a pyramid."

Chris put his hands on his knees and stared at the globe. "Man! That's fantastic!"

"Give me those locations now," Jerry said. Chris handed his grandfather the paper. Jerry rotated the comdat knob, and the hologram of the globe turned slowly. "The first is a mountain 29° longitude east and 63° latitude north." With another knob, he tilted the globe. "That puts it in Finland in the lake country." He peered closely. "I believe the mountain is called Koli."

"Wow!" Chris said. "With all those lakes, that's going to be hard to find."

Jerry studied the paper. "The second is the site of ruins 72° longitude west and 13° latitude south. That's below the equator." He ran his finger down. "Here we are. It's the Inca ruins of Machu Picchu in the Andes."

"Oh, great!" Chris said. "Ever since I learned about that place from the history bank, I've wanted to visit it."

"The third location," Jerry continued, "is a pyramid."

Chris turned the knob. "In Egypt, I'll bet."

"No," Jerry said, turning the knob back. "It's 78° longitude west and 27° latitude north. Hhmm." He examined the globe. "That's funny. That puts the spot in the ocean between Bimini and Andros Island in the Bahamas."

"You know what?" Chris said. "It must be the pyramid that explorers recently located there underwater. I learned about that too."

Jerry nodded. "The area used to be referred to as the Bermuda Triangle."

"It still is," Chris said. "Ships and planes still disappear there mysteriously. We'll need an underwater craft for that job, won't we?"

"Yes." Jerry looked at his grandson. "This is a pretty big order, Chris. Do you still want to help?"

"Sure, if it means going to all those places on Earth. Why not?" He snapped his fingers. "It'll be easy—a piece of carrot cake! Wait till I tell Steve about this!"

Jerry held up his hand. "Just a minute, Chris. Do we want to include Steve in this search?"

"Why, of course. He knows all about Monaal and the reason Earth isn't a member of the Intergalactic Federation yet. He'd be one more pair of eyes to help find the cards."

"All right," Jerry said.

Steve came over and was briefed on the venture. "Wow!" he said. "Monaal really laid it on us! Do you think we can pull it off?"

"Of course!" Chris said, snapping his fingers again. "We'll be heroes!"

"Hey, you two, slow down. This isn't a job to 'pull off.' It's a serious mission." Jerry rubbed his chin. "Can I count on you both not to fool around?"

"Sure, Mr. Cole," Steve said.

"Scout's honor." Chris raised three fingers in a salute.

Steve did the same.

Jerry smiled and saluted back. "You're on," he said.

Steve received permission from his parents to go with Chris and his grandfather on a "fishing trip," as it was labeled.

Chris grinned. "That's really what it is, you know."

During the week that followed, Chris and Steve spent much time in front of Jerry's console. They put on tec-hats, helmets wired to bring the data bank of the computer to the brain's memory bank. They fed into the comdat requests for information about the places they would be visiting, then sat back fascinated as the images flashed into their minds. They could see the places clearly.

Jerry arranged a leave of absence from his work, and within ten days Chris, Jerry, and Steve boarded a shuttle that would land them in Helsinki, Finland. The boys settled back and watched through the shuttle windows as the blue-green planet Earth, with its swirl of clouds, grew larger.

Although the boys were familiar with Earth, Jerry filled them in on what to expect. "You see, boys," he said as he sat across the aisle from them, "years ago, as you know, something had to be done to clean up the air and water on Earth. It was becoming so polluted no one could live there safely. That's why the satellite cities were built. The population was divided between protected domed cities on Earth and the satellite cities orbiting the planet.

"Earth is a very beautiful planet now, with wide green belts of farmland and forests. The rivers, lakes, oceans, and air are clean and pure—no pollutants from factories or fossil fuels." He smiled. "Earth is a great place for vacations."

Chris looked solemn. "But we're sure not on a vacation trip this time." He gazed out the shuttle window. The glint from another craft in space brought his eyes to focus on it. He leaned forward, studying the ship that was rapidly approaching them.

Quickly he laid his hand on Steve's arm. "Look!" He pointed. "Isn't that one of the spacecraft we saw at the way station?"

"Hey, yeah," Steve said. "Do you suppose it's Monaal or one of his representatives come to guide us to the hidden card?"

The elliptical craft drew closer. It paced the Earth shuttle for a short distance. A blue light flashed toward the shuttle. Chris felt a sudden painful tingling in his shoulder.

Then the spacecraft rose, darted over the Earth shuttle, and was gone, but not before Chris saw the emblem underneath.

He felt a chill run through him. The emblem was the letter J with a spear through it!

CHAPTER 3

Cyclo's Warning

Chris rubbed his tingling shoulder and looked at Steve. "Did you see that?"

Steve swallowed. "It was a Jovan emblem. Could it be Cyclo?"

"Who else? With that blue ray he zapped at us, it's got to be Cyclo! That ray must be strong to go right through the shell of this shuttle. Did it get you?"

"A little," Steve said. "My hands tingle."

"So do mine." Chris rubbed his palms together.

Jerry looked anxiously at Chris. "What's this about a blue ray?"

"It comes from a weapon, a black box, that Cyclo carries in front of him."

"Who's Cyclo?"

Chris grimaced. "He's that leader from Jovan I told you about. Remember, the one Monaal had trouble with? Cyclo wants his planet to belong to the Intergalactic Federation, but Monaal says it's not ready yet."

"Yes," Steve added. "Jovan hasn't eliminated war." He frowned. "But why would Cyclo come after us? We're not doing anything to hurt him."

"No?" Chris pointed toward Earth. "We're going down there to find those messages Monaal hid, and Cyclo wants to stop us."

"But why?"

"Can't you see?" Chris asked. "He doesn't want Earth to join the Intergalactic Federation before Jovan does. Remember how he sneered at us at the way station?"

"Sure," Steve said. "Cyclo believes Jovan is light-years ahead of Earth." He rubbed his chin thoughtfully. "How do you suppose he found out about those messages?"

"Look," Chris said, "Jovan's technology is much more advanced than Earth's. There are lots of ways Cyclo could have found out— listened in on Monaal's way station, hooked into computer data lines or microwave transmissions, maybe something we don't even know about yet."

Steve nodded. "He's tricky!"

"You said it! And jealous too. Cyclo could really mess up our search if he wanted to."

Jerry smiled at the boys. "I don't think we need to worry about him. He's only trying to frighten us, not harm us."

Chris shook his head. "You don't know Cyclo!"

The shuttle entered Earth's atmosphere and glided smoothly to a landing at the Helsinki spaceport, a short distance away from the glistening transparent dome of the city. An underground tube-train quickly sucked the three travelers into the climate-controlled city, where they planned to stay the night.

From the balcony of the hotel, Chris looked around at the brightly painted walls and rich wood paneling of the tiered buildings. Slide-walks connected the various levels, where people strolled about or sped along in silent electric glass-walled buses. Beyond the city, through its transparent walls, Chris could see an unbroken landscape of wooded hills, grassy meadows, and stretches of water in the bays and inlets of the seacoast. Finland, Chris decided, would be a great place to go on a Scout trip. He'd have to tell Mr. Bryant about it.

In the morning they left the city and boarded a hover craft that traveled over land and water.

Steve was unusually quiet.

Jerry smiled at him. "What do you think of Planet Earth?"

"I don't know," Steve said. "It's almost scary how far you can see in all directions."

Jerry nodded. "After living all your life in a satellite city where you can see only to the curve of the toroid, this seemingly infinite horizon *can* take some getting used to." He patted Steve's shoulder. "Don't worry. You'll adjust soon enough."

The autumn day passed quickly as the hover craft glided over narrow roads between walls of evergreens, past lush meadows, and across tea-brown lakes that dotted the land. Here and there red and yellow fall leaves hinted of shortening days.

It was late afternoon before they crossed the last lake and approached the domed city of Joensuu in the vicinity of Koli Mountain. They were informed that a small resort was located near the ascent to Koli. The top of the mountain was a flattened dome of rock. It was on this rock that Jerry felt sure the magnetic card was hidden.

Chris looked at his grandfather. "Let's not stay in the city. Let's go up to that resort instead. I've never stayed at a place like that before. Please, may we?"

Jerry hesitated. "I thought we'd stay here so we'd be fresh to tackle that mountain in the morning."

Chris spread his hands. "We can stop at the resort and rest there just as well, can't we?"

"Sure," Steve said. "I'd like to rough it too."

Jerry smiled. "A resort outside a domed city isn't exactly roughing it. But I'll see what I can do. We'll have to rent an electric runabout. Mountain roads are too narrow for the hover craft."

"Great!" Chris and Steve said together.

Jerry called ahead for reservations at the Koli resort. He located a four-seater runabout and piled their gear in the back. Then he guided the car out of the city and onto a winding road walled by tall firs and pines. Shadows lurked among the drooping branches.

Chris looked around. "This would be a good spot for an ambush," he said.

"Ambush!" Steve said. "By whom?"

"Oh, you know." Chris shrugged. "Someone like Cyclo."

"Yeah." Steve grinned. "Old one-eye! I can see him now hiding behind that fir tree over there!"

"Where?" Chris put his hands to his mouth in mock alarm.

Steve pointed to the left as the runabout entered a meadow clearing. Dusk was falling, and Jerry switched on the lights.

He smiled. "Watch it, boys, or you'll scare yourselves."

Chris pointed to his chest. "Who me? Scare myself? That's a laugh!"

Steve pointed again. "See that dot of light on the horizon? It's getting brighter and brighter."

"Sure," Chris said. "That's good old Cyclo coming to chat with us."

"Man!" Steve chuckled as the light disappeared overhead. "Don't you know a meteor when you see one?"

Suddenly the runabout motor died, and the lights went out. Jerry tried to start the car again, but the motor refused to turn over. He groaned. "Wouldn't you know! They gave us a defective runabout."

Chris peered at the dark road ahead. "What do we do now?"

Jerry sighed. "Get out and walk the rest of the way."

"Wait a minute," Steve said. "There must be another car coming. See that light in front of us?"

Chris was aware of the light too. It was coming from above, however, rather than from the road. Abruptly the light went out, and there, staring at them over the runabout hood, hovered the face of Cyclo! His one big eye in the middle of his forehead gleamed cunningly at them. His gray face, with its two slits for a nose and straight line for a mouth, made Chris gasp.

"Greetings." The deep voice of Cyclo oozed from the air about them. "You may remember me from the moon."

"Oh, wow!" Steve breathed. "You were right, Chris!"

"Look," Chris whispered. "I was only kidding. I didn't think…"

The eye drilled into them. "I remember you two small Earthlings well," Cyclo continued. "I know, also, what your mission to Planet Earth is."

"How could you?" Chris asked, though he suspected the answer.

The corners of Cyclo's straight mouth turned up slightly. "Jovan's technology makes that knowledge easily available. The systems of your civilization are so backward."

"Man," Chris said under his breath. "He's disgusting!"

Cyclo went on. "Since you are my—ah—*friends*, I am here to warn you. Easy as your mission may sound, it is a most dangerous one. I advise you not to continue. You will regret it if you do." His face vanished as suddenly as it had appeared.

Steve's voice was husky. "How—how did Cyclo do that?"

Jerry cleared his throat. "By laser beams, I imagine. That was a hologram, like the world globe I have at home. He beamed his image down from his spacecraft, which is probably right above us, and spoke to us through a gismo."

Each of the three stuck his head out of the runabout and stared into the blackness above.

All they could see was a bright light disappearing over the western horizon. They sat quietly in the runabout for a moment.

Jerry broke the silence. "You two had better watch those psychic vibrations of yours. We don't need confrontations like that."

"But I was only kidding," Chris said. "I didn't think Cyclo would really come."

Steve looked at Jerry. "You mean our psychic vibrations brought him here?"

Jerry shrugged. "It's possible. Our minds can play tricks on us sometimes. You two promised me you wouldn't fool around, remember?" He fumbled with the runabout controls. "Now that the spacecraft is gone, this car should start." But the motor still refused to turn over. Even the two-way radio wouldn't work.

"Well, boys," Jerry said, "I guess we start walking." He climbed out of the runabout. "Help me push this thing to the side of the road."

The boys obliged. Then each shouldered a spacecase and started along the dark road toward the resort.

Steve trudged beside Jerry. "Wasn't that a laugh—Cyclo and that bit about being friends?"

"Yeah," Chris said, as he walked on Jerry's other side. "He's about as friendly as a hornet!"

Jerry grinned in the dark. "Look at it this way, boys. Our mission certainly won't be dull with a face like his around."

The boys laughed nervously.

CHAPTER 4

Condition Number One

Chris, Jerry, and Steve arrived at the resort around midnight, having walked eight miles from their disabled runabout. Their rooms were waiting for them, and all three tumbled into bed, exhausted.

The sun was shining brightly the next morning when they awoke. After a hearty breakfast, Jerry notified the rental agency of the disabled car and requested another. Then, with Chris and Steve, he started the easy ascent of Koli. They passed thick groves of firs and restless yellow-leafed aspens. At last they came out onto the great boulder that covered nearly half an acre at the top of Koli.

Chris let out a whistle. "Wow! What a view! Green hills and lakes everywhere."

"Wow is right," Steve said. "From up here, the lakes look blue, but when we crossed them in the hover craft, they were brown. How come?"

Jerry smiled. "We see them reflecting the sky from up here. Down below, we were looking at water stained for years with tannin from the bark of logs floated to the lumber mills." He reached into his coat pocket and drew out three telescoped wands with hinged six-inch metal squares on the bottom. A dial with a needle was built into each square. "Here," he said, handing a wand to each boy. "Use these metal detectors. Watch that needle on the bottom. If it starts to vibrate, you're close to the magnetic card."

Chris looked puzzled. "But aren't the cards plastic?"

"Yes," Jerry said. "But the embossed message on them is metal. That should trigger the needle."

The boys began searching for the inch-square card.

Chris knelt to pass his wand under a ledge of boulder. "It's probably red like the one inside the recorder, right?"

"Could be," Jerry said. "But it might be black, white, or any other color in between."

A dozen people in a tour group arrived, chattering. They spread out over the mountain-top. Some sat down to rest, while others wandered about snapping pictures.

Chris ran his detector along a crevice in the rock.

"What'd you lose, kid?" a plump man with a cigar asked.

"Nothing," Chris said.

"Then stop vandalizing the place. You kids!" The man shook his head. "Got no respect for natural beauty!" He ground out his cigar under his heel, leaving a black mark on the boulder's surface.

Chris glared after the man as the tour group left.

"Hey, you guys," Steve shouted. "I've found it!" Over his head, he waved a black square. It had been wedged under an outer lip of the rock.

Quickly Jerry removed the wrist recorder and replaced the red card with the black one. He pressed the start button. Monaal's high-pitched voice spoke:

"Members of Earth's United Nations:

"We of the Intergalactic Federation have been monitoring your planet, and we feel your progress warrants membership in our organization. You have effectively outlawed war and, in so doing, have directed your resources and energies toward improving the quality of life of all beings on your planet. Within your various countries, you have developed a deep regard for the individual. Also, each country has respect for the next and does not impose its life-style on its neighbor.

"Membership in the Intergalactic Federation opens the door to sharing technologies from planets in other galaxies. These technologies will prove highly beneficial to Earth.

"Three conditions are still necessary, however, before Earth's membership in the Federation can be approved. We present to you now condition number one: You must release from your thinking any sense of ownership of the moons, planets, and asteroids in your galaxy. They are there for all beings in the universe to enjoy, as are all habitable regions. I leave you now to discuss this matter.

"Respectfully, Monaal of Throal Director, Intergalactic Federation."

The recorder hummed a moment and then was silent.

Jerry gazed off into space. "That message has been a long time coming. I remember when I was a boy and Monaal first mentioned that Earth wasn't ready for intergalactic trade yet." He looked at Chris. "Now we *are* ready! Let's get going!"

"Where?" Chris asked.

Jerry grinned. "Why, to the headquarters of the United Nations of Earth in Alpha City. Where else? My fellow members will be going into session tomorrow, and I have to deliver this message to them. It may take me a while to lay the groundwork for all this. After all, only a few of us even know about the Intergalactic Federation."

"Crumb!" Chris said. "I'd hoped we could hang around here for a while. It's a really interesting place."

Jerry patted Chris's shoulder. "We'll remember this location and take a vacation trip here later, the three of us. Okay?"

"Okay," Chris and Steve said together.

* * * *

They arrived back in Alpha City to find the United Nations about to go into session. This Earth-governing body had been moved from New York to the satellite city, a more accessible place for all nations.

Just as the states in the United States were represented in Congress, so all countries on Earth were represented in the United Nations. This once-ineffective body had become a powerful governing force that protected the individual human rights of the citizens in all Earth's countries.

Jerry took Monaal's message to the Secretary General of the U.N. Assembly and explained the Intergalactic Federation to him. The Secretary General agreed with Jerry about the vital importance of joining with Earth's neighbors in space. He put Monaal's message on the agenda for the opening session and declared that the session should be kept secret.

Chris waited impatiently at his grandfather's house for Jerry to return with news of the meeting.

When his grandfather finally arrived, Chris ran to the terrace to meet him. "Did they accept the condition?" he asked eagerly.

Jerry sighed. "Not yet. It'll take some time for many of them just to get used to the idea of inhabited planets united in a space organization. They listened carefully, but then asked that the Assembly be given time to debate the question."

"Debate!" Chris said hotly. "I don't see what there is to debate about such a terrific opportunity. Don't they understand how lucky we are even to be considered *ready* for the Intergalactic Federation? And what's so hard about Monaal's condition?"

"Simmer down, Chris," Jerry said, patting his grandson's shoulder. "It isn't easy for people to accept new ideas and to change their attitudes about ownership. It has taken us many years and much work to develop the technology necessary to reach the moons, asteroids, and planets near us. It's only logical that some people still have a possessive attitude toward these places."

"But that's such old-fashioned thinking. It's like what they used to do—one nation planting its flag on the moon and saying, 'Hey, this is mine. Keep off.' That went out ages ago."

"True, Chris. But just as it took time for nations to realize they must share this planet if they hope to survive, so it will take some thought for the United Nations to accept Monaal's condition about sharing other bodies in space. Don't worry, though. I'm sure the Assembly is responsible enough to make the right decision. Meanwhile, they've given me a leave to find that second card in the Andes."

"Great!" Chris said. "That's a place I've always wanted to see too. When do we leave?"

"Tomorrow we start for Machu Picchu!"

CHAPTER 5

Meeting at Machu Picchu

On arriving at his grandparents' house, Chris had found a message from Mr. Bryant. The troop was holding a meeting that evening to evaluate its performance on the moon.

Chris didn't want to go, but Jerry insisted. "Look," Chris said, "all Bryant is going to do is give Steve and me the axe."

"I don't believe so," his grandfather said. "He may criticize your behavior, but I don't think he'll expel you from the troop."

"But he'll want to know what happened, what we saw, and all that stuff. What can we tell him?"

"You shouldn't discuss the way station, of course, but you might mention a few things that would satisfy Mr. Bryant's curiosity. You can keep faith with Monaal and at the same time be courteous to your Scoutmaster. It'll take some self-control, but I know you and Steve can do it."

Chris and Steve cycled to the Scout meeting. The boys edged in the door and sat at the back of the room until Mr. Bryant saw them and motioned for them to come up front. The other Scouts were eager to share their moon experiences.

At last it was Chris's turn to talk. He glanced at Steve and stood up. "All I can say is that Steve and I—we got lost." He sat down.

Mr. Bryant frowned. "Surely you had *some* experiences during those three days. What did you see?"

Chris shrugged. "Just some spacecraft from other galaxies."

A few Scouts snickered.

Mr. Bryant held up his hand. "Boys, no laughing. Let Chris continue. What did they look like?"

"Elliptical, like flying saucers. They had emblems underneath."

"Yes," Steve said. "One had the letter J with a spear through it."

Mr. Bryant smiled nervously. "Now, see? You two did have an experience. Observing alien spacecraft on the moon, or anywhere else for that matter, is an experience. For years people have been claiming to see such craft." He looked sober. "I trust you really *did* see such craft. A Scout that fabricates—"

Chris's anger began to rise. "Mr. Bryant," he said, "we did see alien spacecraft! If you don't believe me, ask my grandfather. He's seen them too. And all of you are going to see them when—when—"

Chris stopped suddenly. He must watch himself, or he would give their secret mission away.

"Yeah? When?" a Scout asked.

Chris looked desperately at Steve. It was hard to hold in his feelings when the others were making fun of him. "When Earth's government learns to share our galaxy with others in the universe, that's when!"

"He's right," Steve said.

The Scouts began to laugh.

Mr. Bryant held up his hand again for quiet. "That's an interesting theory, Chris, but hard to prove, isn't it?"

Chris swallowed. Jerry had said it would take self-control to handle this situation. He'd have to be careful how he answered the Scoutmaster. "It will be proved, you'll see. I have faith."

Steve nodded.

* * * *

The following day Chris, Steve, and Jerry, in an Earth shuttle, were hurtling through space toward Lima, Peru. The boys kept an anxious eye out for Cyclo's spaceship all the way, but it didn't materialize. They breathed easier as they climbed out of the shuttle at the spaceport.

Lima, like Helsinki, was a city constructed within a gigantic transparent dome. The three visitors would have liked to explore it, but there was no time. Within hours they were skimming over the Andes in a sleek and silent stub-winged plane propelled by magnetic-solar power.

They arrived at the ancient city of Cuzco, which stood, as it had for centuries, in the well-watered Cuzco Valley. It was preserved as a historic landmark with no dome covering it.

Cobblestoned streets in the old quarters wandered through narrow passageways. Massive stone walls, built by the Incas centuries ago, rose here and there as foundations for the Spanish-style buildings.

Chris and Steve found it hard not to stare at the Quechua Indians, who wore their traditional gay-colored woolens as they squatted in the open market. Beside them lay piles of corn and potatoes for sale.

"You know something?" Chris said to his grandfather. "I didn't realize people still lived like this. I feel as though I've stepped back into history."

Jerry smiled. "You have, in a way. These people prefer to live as their ancestors did. And now, with each country respecting the other, people are entitled to live as they choose, provided they aren't endangering their neighbors."

Chris nodded. "That's the way it is in the Intergalactic Federation too. Monaal told us about it."

The next morning Jerry received permission from the authorities to camp at Machu Picchu for a few days. He hired a small solar-powered aircraft. It was designed to fly a few hundred feet above the ground, operating on an automatic pilot hooked into computer-controlled traffic lanes. Jerry helped the boys load their camping gear into the craft, then set the controls for the Urubamba River, which led to the mountaintop ruins of Machu Picchu.

The boys stared in awe at the swift river that tumbled noisily below them. On either side rose steep mountains shrouded in thick jungle growth. They reached, at last, the sheer walls of granite on top of which lay the ancient city of the Incas.

The aircraft rose slowly to the summit. Chris sucked in his breath as the white granite walls of the fabled city stretched away, climbing the narrow ridge of the mountain. He looked in wonder at Jerry. "I didn't know it was *that* big, did you?"

The aircraft came to rest on a broad stretch of grass below the main city. A herd of llamas grazed nearby.

Jerry shook his head. "This is going to take some hunting, I can tell you!"

Steve sighed. "If you ask me, it's going to be impossible to find an inch-square magnetic card in a place like this!"

They climbed out of the aircraft. Jerry reached in for the camping gear.

"Here's your opportunity to rough it, boys," he said, handing Chris and Steve their sleeping bags. "We'll set up camp over in the shelter of that three-sided ruin."

Chris and Steve ran toward the area.

"Take it easy," Jerry called after them. "We're more than two thousand meters above sea level here. There's not as much oxygen at this height as there is in Alpha City, so slow down."

Chris soon learned what Jerry was talking about. He found himself puffing as he climbed a series of steps leading to the highest temple in the city. From there, he surveyed the mountains that rose on either side like monstrous green dragon teeth. He could hear, faintly from below, the roar of the Urubamba rushing toward the Amazon River.

"How could anyone live in an isolated place like this?" he said to Jerry, who was sitting on a stone wall to catch his breath.

Jerry pointed. "Do you see those terraced mountainsides?"

Chris and Steve observed the narrow rock retaining walls that climbed the steep mountain in a neat staircase.

"The Incas," Jerry continued, "grew corn and potatoes and other produce on them. Water came from springs in that mountain above and was channeled down through rock aqueducts to fountains in the city. That way, the people could survive."

"Yes, I know," Chris said. "I tuned in on the history bank. What I mean is, how could anyone stand to be stuck here all the time? There wasn't any aircraft to take them anywhere."

Jerry chuckled. "If the Incas who lived here could see what we have today, they'd think they were dreaming. But enough about the past. What we're concerned with now is how to find Monaal's second magnetic card. How about this plan?"

Jerry drew a rough sketch of the city on a note pad. They agreed about where each one would hunt. But by nightfall they had covered only a small portion of the white granite ruins.

They gathered around the small campfire made from llama chips, ate their supper, and sat watching the stars come out.

With the darkness, Chris began to feel uneasy. "There's something about this place that gives me the creeps," he said as he zipped up his jacket. "Does it do that to you, Steve?"

"Sure," Steve said. "It's a spooky feeling, as if an Inca might step out from behind that wall over there at any minute."

"Yeah," Chris said.

Jerry poked the fire. "We'd better turn in early, kids. We have a big city out there to explore tomorrow."

Chris rolled out his sleeping bag. "Darn!" he muttered. "I left my toothbrush and junk in the aircraft. Want to go with me to get them?"

"Sure," Steve said, and they started off.

The farther they walked from the campfire, however, the more uneasy Chris felt. They had to pass around several stone walls before they came to the clearing where the aircraft stood, shadowy in the light from the brilliant stars overhead.

Chris had retrieved his bag, and they were heading back to the campfire when a glow from behind a stone wall directly in front of them grew brighter and brighter.

Steve clutched Chris's arm, and they halted.

Chris leaned close to Steve. "You suppose Jerry poked up the fire and it's reflecting behind that wall?"

Steve shook his head. "I think it's an Inca ghost or something!"

"Come on! There aren't any ghosts around here!"

"Oh, no? Look at that!" Steve pointed.

From behind the wall, the figure of a tall man emerged slowly. It was luminous and hard to define. Gradually the outline grew clearer.

"Greetings, my friends!" The voice was unmistakable.

"Oh no, Steve!" Chris exclaimed. "It's Cyclo!"

CHAPTER 6

A Circle of Danger

The boys stood staring at the silvery figure of Cyclo. A gismo hung on a cord around his neck, and from a black box on his chest blinked the menacing blue light.

"So," Cyclo said, putting his hands on his hips and glaring at them with his one large eye, "you do not believe me, I see."

Chris gulped. "Believe you about what?" he asked.

Cyclo pointed a long index finger at the two boys. "That this mission of yours is highly dangerous."

"Look, Cyclo," Chris said, "what's it to you if Earth's government joins the Intergalactic Federation?"

Cyclo appeared to grow taller than his seven feet. "Our planet Jovan is superior in every way to Earth. We have every right to be admitted to the Federation before your—your primitive planet!"

Steve spoke up. "But Monaal says you still settle *your* problems with war. That's about as primitive as you can get."

"War is necessary!" Cyclo said. "It is part of the nature of all beings, no matter what planet they live on!"

"I disagree!" It was Jerry speaking. Chris could see his grandfather had come up behind Cyclo. Jerry continued, "A warlike nature may have been part of a being's attitude to *start* with, but such an attitude can be overcome."

Cyclo wheeled about. "So! An Earthling tells a Jovanian that war is not necessary—*you*, who destroyed your earliest cultures and nearly eliminated life on your planet with nuclear war!"

"True," Jerry said. "But we caught ourselves this last time just before that happened. It's a struggle, Cyclo, to bring countries together, to control distrust, to stamp out fear. But we've done it!"

Chris seized Steve's arm. "Look," he whispered. "You can see Jerry right through Cyclo."

"Yeah," Steve said. "How come?"

"Because that isn't Cyclo!"

"What do you mean?"

Chris leaned close. "That's another hologram of him—just like the last time, when he beamed his face in front of our runabout in

Finland. Look. I'll prove it." Chris walked toward Cyclo. "Hey, Cyclo," he said, "you're nothing but a bag of hot air!"

Cyclo turned to face Chris. He touched the black box. "I'm warning you, Earthling! I shall be forced to stop you with this ray."

"Oh?" Chris said. "Try it! Come on, Steve, we've got to get back to camp."

Steve hesitated. "But he'll zap us with that blue light!"

"No, he won't. That's just an image of one. The ray won't work unless it's the real thing."

Chris ran at Cyclo, closing his eyes for a second as he passed through the image. He felt a slight heat, but nothing else. With his eyes open, he ran toward Jerry.

His grandfather grabbed his hand. "Nice work, Chris. I wondered how long it would be before you realized it wasn't the real Cyclo."

Chris turned to look. The image was gone. Overhead a dark round shadow was sliding rapidly away into the night. Chris let out a big sigh. "Man! That bag of hot air doesn't give up, does he!"

Jerry patted Chris's shoulder as the three of them trudged back to camp. "So far," he said, "Cyclo has been all bluff. But we mustn't let our guard down. Whether he means to or not, he could still live up to his threat and make this mission a dangerous one."

Steve looked at Jerry. "Like killing us?"

Jerry shook his head. "I doubt that."

"Why not?" Steve asked. "He could zap us easy."

"If he did that," Jerry said, "he might anger Monaal."

Chris spoke up. "But Monaal doesn't get angry."

"Maybe not," Jerry said, "but if Monaal found out Cyclo had destroyed us, Cyclo's chances of bringing his planet into the Intergalactic Federation would be lost forever."

Chris nodded. "Yes, I guess so."

He shivered for a moment. Was it from the cold night air settling into the ground or from this last encounter with Cyclo? He wasn't sure.

Jerry smiled down at him. "How about a cup of hot chocolate before we turn in?"

That sounded good to everyone, and steaming cups were soon ready.

Chris sipped the warm drink and wondered if Monaal was aware of Cyclo's interference. Perhaps if Monaal had kept Cyclo out of circulation for a while, all of this wouldn't be happening. But Monaal couldn't seem to see the bad in anybody. Still, he didn't approve of war and greed and untrustworthy people. Why couldn't he see that Cyclo was dangerous?

Warm in his sleeping bag, Chris wondered what Cyclo might try next. He stared at the brilliant stars overhead. Were any of them in Cyclo's galaxy? he wondered. Where was Throal, the planet Monaal came from? Those millions of stars overhead were suns around which innumerable planets revolved. Many of them were inhabited. How important that Earth become a member of this universal family! He fell asleep wondering which galaxies out there would soon be Earth's friends.

The next morning Jerry awakened the boys early. "We have a whole city to explore," he said. "And the sooner we start, the better. We can't move as quickly up here where there's less oxygen, and it will be very hot by noon."

Chris, Steve, and Jerry once again trudged up the steep stone stairways, clambered over massive stone walls, and poked about in the crevices of roofless granite houses. They met a few tourists who had arrived by aircraft at the reception center nearby.

By noon Chris, wiping his sweaty forehead, collapsed in the shadow of a stone wall. Steve joined him, shaking his head.

"This is impossible," Steve said. "How can we find an inch-square card in ruins this size?"

Jerry arrived and handed each boy a small tube of concentrated lunch. They removed the caps and sucked at the contents, a high-protein combination that tasted like corned beef on rye. No one said much for a while.

Finally Jerry spoke. "I think we should look more closely at Monaal's directions again. I'm sure he would have planned this location carefully and given us clues of some kind." He drew from his pocket the message Chris had copied from the computer at home. He handed it to Chris. "You reviewed the information on these ruins before we came here. Do you see anything in the message that might give us a clue?"

Chris studied the paper. "All I see is that triangle of dots with a circle beside it." He passed the paper to Steve.

Steve looked up. "The triangle stands for ruins, right? What does the circle beside it stand for?"

Chris shrugged. "For degrees, doesn't it?"

Jerry reached for the paper. "Not necessarily. That circle might stand for the sun."

Chris looked puzzled. "What would the sun have to do with it?"

Jerry folded the paper and stood up. "I think I know. There are two places in the ruins that have to do with the sun. There's a temple near the highest point in the city where the priests were said to tie the sun to a stake at the summer solstice, the longest day of the year. Actually, the sun went directly behind a certain stone at that time, and the idea was to keep the sun from slipping away."

Chris jumped up. "I remember the other place now! The circular Sun Temple! The sun shines through a window and covers a certain raised stone completely at the winter solstice, the shortest day of the year."

Jerry grinned. "Right!"

Chris continued. "I should have thought of the place you mentioned, Jerry. It's called the Hitching Post of the Sun, and it's up there." He pointed toward a long flight of steps leading to an elevated temple.

The three hurried to the temple and found the Hitching Post of the Sun. Although they searched every inch of the stone and its base, there was no sign of the magnetic card.

"Well," Chris said, "it's not here—that's for sure. Let's try the Sun Temple."

The circular stone wall of the Sun Temple curved around the top of a huge outcropping of granite. Cool dark recesses lay under the rock. Chris wondered if there could have been tombs under here as there had been elsewhere under boulders.

They searched every bit of the circular wall. Chris stood gazing down at the raised stone in the center of the room. The sunlight covered only part of it now. He crouched on his heels to examine more closely the shaded portions of the rock. He started to run his hand around the shadowed part, then withdrew it. The stone felt damp and rough there.

He peered closely at the head of the rock. A small circular object lay close to it on the shaded floor. In the center was a familiar square, green this time.

Chris knew at once this was the magnetic card. "Hey, you guys," he shouted, "I've found it!" He started to reach for the card, then drew his hand back in horror.

The object encircling the card was the slender body of a deadly viper!

CHAPTER 7

The Second Message

Chris stared at the dark body of the snake coiled around the green card. Here was the message they had sought for two days, guarded by a viper! Was this one of Cyclo's tricks? No, if Cyclo knew the card was here, he would have taken it.

Chris looked at Jerry. "What do we do now?"

Jerry held up a warning hand. "Don't touch it!" He looked around. "See if you two can find a stick so we can move the viper away."

Chris and Steve hurried outside. Hunt as they would, however, they could find no sticks or tree branches on the grass-covered ground, and they returned to Jerry.

"Look," Jerry said, "all we need to do is persuade this fellow to go elsewhere."

"Hey, I know," Chris said. "If we push one of our knapsacks toward it, that might scare it away. I'll go get mine." Chris hurried off.

His suggestion worked, and the snake slithered into one of the cracks between the stones of the temple.

Chris picked up the green card and handed it to his grandfather. "Play it, Jerry," he said.

In the shade of the Sun Temple walls, Jerry slipped the card into his wrist recorder. Monaal's voice came through:

"Here is the second condition for the members of the United Nations of Earth to consider.

"In your future exploration of space, you must have respect for those forms of life different from your own. Environments differ from

one habitable planet, moon, or asteroid to the next. Life forms de-velop that best suit their environments. You must respect these vary-ing life forms and refrain from tampering with them. Are you willing to do this? I leave you to discuss this second condition.

"This is Monaal of Throal wishing you well."

Chris looked at Steve. "That shouldn't be hard to do."

Steve looked thoughtful. "I don't know. Remember Gat at the way station, with his hairy body and long arms and hands with claws?"

"Sure," Chris said, smiling. He looked at Jerry. "Gat was this incredible person we worked with on the moon. He said the pressure on his planet of Felson was so great that beings there developed a carapace—like a turtle shell—under their skin."

"Well," Steve continued, "it took us a while to get used to Gat, didn't it?"

"Yes," Chris said. "But Monaal isn't asking the United Nations of Earth to get cozy with aliens right away. He's just saying that Earth people must respect them and not try to change them. Right, Jerry?"

"Right," Jerry said. "Now we'd better make tracks for the aircraft and head back to Alpha City."

They retraced their way to Cuzco, to Lima, and finally to the shuttle that sped them to their satellite city.

At the United Nations Assembly, Jerry presented the second con-dition.

Chris questioned his grandfather on his return. "What did they decide about Monaal's first message? What did they say about this one?"

Jerry smiled. "They were quite positive, but they want to hear all the conditions before committing themselves."

"Crumb! Why can't they decide on each message as you deliver it?"

"I told you, Chris—it takes time. They want to be sure before they make such a momentous decision." He smiled at his grandson. "Have a little patience, pal."

"Well, when do we leave to find the last message?"

"In a few days," Jerry said. "I have a space colony on Asteroid 94 to check out first."

While Chris and Steve were waiting for Jerry's return, Mr. Bry-ant urged them to attend a Scout meeting one afternoon at the Alpha

City Recreation Center. It was located in the hub of the great wheel, where gravity was near zero and weightlessness made every sport fun. Chris and Steve welcomed the invitation; the outing would make their wait go faster.

The troop divided into two teams and played volleyball. Chris leaped six feet into the air, hit the ball, and turned a slow somersault as he returned to the floor. Steve, nearby, was trying to get his balance as he floated to one side.

Chris laughed as Steve, feet in the air, tried to hit the ball as it floated near him. The ball glanced off his head and deflected in a straight line to the ceiling, then in another straight line over the net. "That's using the old bean, Steve," Chris said and struggled to stay upright himself.

He had to smile at Mr. Bryant, who was keeping score. The Scoutmaster clung to the pole that held the volleyball net in place, his feet floating upward. If Mr. Bryant let go, Chris knew, he would float to the ceiling.

During a rest break, the Scouts sipped soft drinks from squeeze bottles. The talk turned to their recent trip.

One boy said to Chris and Steve, "You guys must have had a wild time out there on the moon all by yourselves."

"Yes," another agreed. "Seeing flying saucers and everything. You sure you weren't dreaming?"

Chris glanced at Steve. The others would tease him until he got mad and told them the true story. He mustn't let that happen. He shrugged. "Maybe we were, and maybe we weren't. Does it matter to you?"

The boys looked at one another.

"Well," one said, "Bryant sure thinks so."

Chris tossed the volleyball into the air and watched it float toward the ceiling. "So? He wasn't there to see those saucers, and we were. Now, come on, you guys. Let's play another game." He leaped into the air and caught the ball as it deflected from the ceiling.

The other Scouts disposed of their squeeze bottles and joined him. Chris winked at Steve. He had managed once more to keep from telling their secret.

* * * *

It was early one morning a week later that Chris, Steve, and Jerry boarded another shuttle to Earth. This time their destination was Miami Beach on the North American continent.

Chris watched through the shuttle window as the blue Atlantic Ocean grew closer and closer. Then he asked Jerry, "How do we get to the Bahamas?"

"We take an aircraft from Miami to Nassau." Jerry pointed. "Look down, boys. See that light-colored water surrounding the Bahama Banks? The land around those islands is slowly rising again."

"Oh, yes," Chris said. "I heard about it. That's where some people believe the lost continent of Atlantis used to be."

"Really? How do they figure that?" Steve asked.

"Easy," Chris said. "All kinds of stone-paved roads, piers, and plazas have been uncovered. Temples too."

"And," Jerry added, "that's where some archaeologists recently discovered a great pyramid larger than any in Egypt."

"Wow!" Steve said.

Chris sat back. "Monaal has hidden the last card on that underwater pyramid." He looked over at Jerry. "Are we going to use diving gear to find the card?"

Jerry smiled. "No, the pyramid is too deep for that. I've ordered a small underwater retrieval craft. There'll be room in it for the three of us, and it has movable exterior arms we can manipulate from inside."

"Neat!" Chris said. He turned to Steve. "Did you know they call that area down there the Bermuda Triangle?"

"Sure," Steve said. "I've read some spooky stories about it." He looked at Jerry. "Is it safe to go down there?"

Jerry smiled. "I don't think we need to worry about it. There's probably a logical explanation for the unusual things that happen there."

Steve shivered. "I hope they don't happen to us."

* * * *

The next morning they boarded a small aircraft and, with four other passengers, left Miami for the Bahamas. The sky was clear; the water below, a deep bright blue. Chris's spirits rose with the plane. The third and last card was almost theirs.

Chris looked out the window. That was strange! A thick cloud of phosphorescent green lay just ahead of them. Where had it come from? The aircraft entered the green cloud and stayed in it for a long time—much longer, it seemed to Chris, than it should take them to reach Nassau.

Suddenly the plane began to vibrate. An oppressive silence descended over everything. Peering down the aisle, Chris could see the pilot and copilot exchanging concerned gestures. The copilot kept calling on the communications system and listening intently for an answer. Chris felt his heart begin to beat faster. The craft was descending rapidly.

The intercom crackled with the pilot's voice. "I regret to inform you that we have lost our power and are losing altitude. We'll be forced to evacuate the plane. We have radioed our position. Please stay calm, everyone. Rescue boats should be here soon. Life preservers are located under your seats. Take them out and put them on; then refasten your seat belts. We expect the plane to stay afloat long enough for us to inflate our three rubber life rafts. Again, I urge you, please stay calm." His voice snapped off.

Chris gulped and looked across at Jerry. This was something they hadn't anticipated—an aircraft crash in the Bermuda Triangle!

CHAPTER 8

Lost in the Bermuda Triangle

Great fans of water flew in all directions as the plane struck the ocean surface. Fearfully, the passengers scrambled from their seats and onto the wings of the sinking plane. In the strange gray-green fog that surrounded them, they climbed into the three life rafts the pilot and copilot had inflated for them.

Chris, Steve, and Jerry bobbed about in one rubber boat, while the pilot, copilot, and four passengers divided up between the other two rafts. It was impossible for the three boats to stay together, even with people using the small paddles fastened to the other rescue gear. The fog swallowed up the rafts as great ocean swells lifted the light crafts onto crests and dropped them like bobbing corks into the troughs.

Chris watched anxiously as the other life rafts disappeared behind another mountain of water. He glanced at Jerry. "Oceans sure look different close up," he said.

Jerry worked the paddle. "How so?"

"Oh, you know," Chris said. "They're not so scary-looking from up in the air as they are down here."

Jerry rested a moment. "There's nothing to be afraid of as long as we keep our heads." He shaded his eyes with one hand and squinted into the fog. "There'll be a rescue ship or plane along soon. We can't be too far from land."

Steve spoke up. "Are you going to use the rescue flares now?"

"No," Jerry said. "We'd better wait until the fog clears."

Within an hour the fog began to melt away. The hot sun beat down on Chris's head.

He had lost sight completely of the other two life rafts. It was hard to keep from showing his rising fear when all he could see around him were heaving swells of endless ocean.

Night came at last, bringing relief from the sun's heat. Chris gazed up at the cool stars studding the sky. He wondered where Alpha City was now. Even with Jerry and Steve beside him, he had never felt so alone before in his life. He wished he were home safe in his bed. He closed his eyes for a moment. Something made him open them again.

One of the stars above appeared to be moving closer. Was it his own Satellite City Alpha? No, it couldn't be. The light was growing larger and larger. In a few minutes it resolved into a round spacecraft that hovered over them.

"Look, Jerry! Steve!" Chris exclaimed, pointing at the spacecraft bobbing gently above them.

"Man!" Steve said. "Do you suppose that's Monaal come to rescue us?"

"Let's hope so," Jerry said. "It looks like his spaceship I saw years ago."

A round opening appeared in the bottom of the craft, and a spotlight beamed down on the water. The craft maneuvered until the light fell directly on the boat. Chris felt himself suddenly rising into the air. He was being beamed into the spacecraft. He could see Jerry and Steve following him up.

The light inside the craft was brilliant. Chris put his arms over his eyes to shield them for a moment. The opening below his feet slid shut, and Chris, blinking, looked around. Jerry and Steve stood beside him. A large console filled one wall of the craft. The figure at the controls turned slowly.

Chris drew in his breath. It wasn't Monaal. It was Cyclo!

The Jovanian leaned back in his contoured seat, the blue fight on his chest winking. "You Earthlings still believe this mission isn't dangerous?" he said.

Chris frowned. "Did you wreck that aircraft?"

Cyclo waved a hand. "There was no need for me to do that. The crystal still buried in the Atlantian pyramid was the cause of your accident." He smiled. "If you Earthlings ever learn to harness that crystal's power, you'll advance a century overnight." He stood up. "But there's no chance of that. You stupidly argue that Atlantis never existed at all, while below your ocean lie the remains of a power source that once beamed aircraft into space."

Chris looked at Jerry. "Is he talking about that underwater pyramid we came to find?"

"Could be," Jerry said.

Steve spoke up. "What are you going to do with us, Cyclo?"

Cyclo cocked his head. "That depends."

"On what?" Steve asked.

"On your cooperation. Abandon this foolish mission, and I will return you to land."

Chris bristled at Cyclo's words. "This mission isn't foolish!"

Jerry laid a hand on Chris's arm. "What my grandson means is that we feel Monaal's requests for a few changes in Earth's policies are worth the effort, if it will admit us to the Intergalactic Federation. We're going to pursue our mission."

"Bah!" Cyclo glowered at them with his large eye. "Only the weak governments pay any attention to Monaal's demands." He turned toward the control panel. "Your refusal to cooperate leaves me no choice."

The opening in the floor appeared, and Chris felt himself drawn over it. In a second he was plummeting toward the ocean. He hit the black water with a splash and came up sputtering near the rubber raft.

He swam toward it as Jerry and Steve followed him into the water. With a swish, the spacecraft sped away into the night sky.

The three managed to climb into the boat again. They sat wet and shivering as they bobbed to the top of one black swell and down again.

Steve looked at Jerry. "You said Cyclo wouldn't try to kill us. He came pretty close to doing it just now."

"I don't think so," Jerry said. "He dropped us right by our raft, didn't he?"

"Sure," Chris said. "He could have dumped us somewhere else."

"Maybe," Steve said and shivered. "If he's only bluffing, he's getting darned good at it. What do you suppose he'll try next?"

Jerry drew the boys close to him. "A little combined body heat here will take some of these shivers away. And let's stop thinking about Cyclo. Most bluffers are trying to cover up their fear of something."

Steve sniffed. "Not Cyclo!"

"Why not?" Jerry said. "I think he's afraid that what he stands for—wars to settle a planet's problems—isn't effective anymore."

"Not effective!" Steve said. "Wars mess up everything, don't they?"

"Yes, and the problems of greed, selfishness, intolerance, and appetite for power don't go away. Like weeds, they have to be rooted out before people can learn to get along with one another."

Chris leaned against Jerry. "You know, I feel kind of sorry for Cyclo. He wants so much to belong to the Intergalactic Federation."

"Well, I don't feel sorry for him!" Steve said.

Jerry squeezed the boys' shoulders. "Let's forget Cyclo, fellows, and try to get some sleep."

* * * *

Dawn streaked the sky. They awoke to find the water around them a slate gray. A freighter's outline appeared to the east. Quickly Jerry sent up the rescue flares. It looked for a few minutes as though the freighter would pass them by. But soon Chris could see it was changing course. Its hull loomed larger and larger.

It wasn't until they were within shouting range that Chris spied a black fin cutting the water close by. Another fin, and still another, circled their rubber raft. He gulped. Sharks! Had they been out there all the time? It was a good thing he hadn't noticed them before. That was all he would have needed to panic.

Jerry, paddling furiously, brought the boat next to the freighter. There were a few anxious moments as the crew lowered the rescue basket. One of the sharks slid between the rubber raft and the freighter, temporarily separating the two craft.

Chris, Jerry, and Steve soon entered the rescue basket, however, and were hauled aboard the freighter. They peered down. Wide-eyed, Chris watched as the nose of a large shark came up under the rubber boat and tipped it over.

"Oh, wow!" he breathed. "Did you see that?"

Steve gulped and nodded. "That was close!"

"Well," Jerry said, "Cyclo may be right about this mission being dangerous. But we can't blame *him* for the sharks!"

From the freighter's captain, they learned that their plane had overshot the Bahamas when its instruments went out of control. The occupants of the other two life rafts had been picked up the day before by a sailing craft. Everyone was safe.

Relieved and happy, the three passengers followed the captain to his quarters. There they enjoyed a hot meal and a few hours of sleep before the freighter docked at Nassau.

Then, after many warm handshakes and thank-yous, Jerry and the boys left the ship and headed toward the station where Jerry had arranged for an underwater retrieval craft. They entered the craft, secured the doors, and submerged slowly.

"Hey, look," said Steve, peering through one of the portholes. "The water's so clear you can see for miles. Which way is the pyramid?"

Jerry nodded at the map beside the control panel and traced their planned route with one finger. "The pyramid's located in the waters between the islands of Bimini and Andros. We'll be there in no time."

Chris was the first to see the underwater ruins. He stared at the submerged stone streets, platforms, and walls. Brightly colored fish swam among the fallen temple columns that lay scattered about the floor of the ocean. Once covered by sand, these columns were gradually emerging as the land rose.

The pyramid itself was in much deeper water. Still, there was no mistaking its shape. Chris looked in awe as the green sunlight from above rippled across its sharp angles. There was a luminous quality at the very top of the pyramid. Could that be caused by the crystal Cyclo had mentioned?

Slowly, Jerry cruised around the top of the pyramid. "Keep your eyes peeled for the inch-square card," he said. "It's probably in a waterproof container of some kind."

On the fourth turn around the pyramid, Jerry whistled. "There it is! I see it!"

"Where?" Chris and Steve said together.

"There. On that narrow ledge just below the top." The boys peered intently as Jerry pointed. "It must be in that silver-colored box. See?"

Chris spied it. "I see! Now, how do we get it?"

Jerry manipulated one of the mechanical arms attached to the outside of the craft. "This should do it," he said.

The pincers on the end of the arm opened as Jerry moved a lever on the control panel.

The pincers lifted the container from the ledge. "Hey," Chris said. "That was neat!" Hardly had he spoken, however, when the container slipped from the mechanical hand. Chris watched in dismay as the silver box eddied slowly toward the black depths below.

CHAPTER 9

In the Hands of the U.N.

Jerry acted quickly. Pointing the retrieval craft sharply downward, he extended the second arm with its basketlike hand. Chris clenched his fists and held his breath. Would they lose the magnetic-card container in the darkness below?

The silver-colored box struck the expanding side of the pyramid and bounced upward for a moment. Jerry worked a second lever, and the mechanical arm extended farther, opening its basket-hand. The silver container arched gently into the basket. Jerry pressed a button and brought the top edges of the net basket together. The card was safe!

Chris let out his breath. "Whew! That was too close!"

"You said it!" Steve exclaimed.

Jerry smiled as he headed back to port. "Who was the guy that said this mission would be easy?"

Chris grinned. "A guy can change his mind, can't he? Besides, I hadn't counted on Cyclo interfering."

Steve nodded. "Or having a plane wreck and being attacked by sharks."

Chris frowned. "We weren't really attacked by sharks."

Steve shrugged. "Well, we could have been, if that freighter hadn't rescued us in time."

"Look, boys," Jerry said. "That's all behind us. Now it's on to Alpha City and the United Nations of Earth. My concern is what the government's decision will be." He pointed out the window at the basket trailing from the mechanical arm. "The condition on that last card is going to be crucial."

It wasn't until they were on board the Earth shuttle headed for Alpha City that Jerry could play the card. It was a blue one this time. Chris and Steve crowded around Jerry as he placed it in his wrist recorder. Monaal's clear voice spoke:

"Members of Earth's United Nations:

"This is the third and most important condition you are to consider for membership in the Intergalactic Federation. Once you become a member, communications and trade systems will be set up between your planet and participating galaxies. You will have frequent contact with beings who may differ in outward appearance from yourselves. You must regard these beings as your equals, giving them the same respect you give individuals on your own planet.

Now that you have heard the three conditions, I hope you find them satisfactory and will wish to join us. If so, please draw up a written document to this effect and sign it. Jerry Cole, Chris Cole, and Steve Gregg will deliver this document to us. If Earth's United Nations agrees to all three conditions, we will immediately send envoys to welcome you into the Intergalactic Federation.

"This is Monaal of Throal, looking forward to your answer."

"Hey," Chris said, "that shouldn't be hard for the Assembly to decide."

Jerry looked thoughtful. "I don't know. They might agree to join if the members of the United Nations of Earth knew Monaal as we do. If they had learned to work with beings different in appearance from themselves, as you and Steve have, I'm sure they wouldn't hesitate to vote in favor. But this is all very new to them. It may take some time for them to decide, so don't be impatient, you two."

* * * *

Jerry was right. When he delivered the third message to the United Nations Assembly, the discussion about joining the Intergalactic Federation grew long and heated. It lasted well into the night, and the decision was postponed until the next day.

As Jerry prepared the following morning to return to the Assembly, Chris asked, "What is it that's holding up the Assembly's decision?

Are they afraid of getting involved or of losing some rights?"

Jerry shook his head. "No. It's something else. I think the whole idea of associating with beings superior in knowledge to us is frightening to some of the delegates."

Chris spread his hands. "Why should that be? After working with beings like Monaal and Gat, I didn't feel afraid. I realized they knew more than I did, but that didn't change things. They were my friends."

Jerry smiled. "But weren't you a little startled at first? I'm sure I would have been. And that's what bothers some of the delegates."

"Sure, I guess it took a little time getting used to Gat. But he was great once you got to know him."

Jerry put on his jacket. "So have patience, Chris. If the Assembly feels this isn't the time to join the Federation, it will have to be later. Nothing will be lost."

Chris clenched his fists. "But something *will* be lost—Monaal's faith in us! Please, Jerry, can't you show them that once we make contact with other beings, Earth will start to grow outward? That's where I want to be someday—going to other galaxies where I'll be welcome, learning new things, meeting new beings, bringing new ideas back to my planet. Don't you want that too, Jerry?"

His grandfather put his hands on Chris's shoulders. "Of course I do. And I agree with Monaal. Someday you'll be a leader representing this planet." He smiled. "And now, with your pep talk in mind,

I'm off to the United Nations to bring Earth into the Intergalactic Federation!"

Chris grinned at his grandfather. "You show 'em, Jerry!"

* * * *

After three days of debate, the United Nations Assembly finally passed the resolution to join the Intergalactic Federation.

The documents took a few days to prepare and sign. Then, with handshakes and good wishes, the Secretary General and the other delegates saw Jerry off, accompanied by Chris and Steve. The three envoys left in a special shuttle to the moon, with two pilots as the only other people aboard.

Chris was excited as they neared the moon. "Well, Jerry," he said, "we're almost home free!"

"Oh-oh," Steve said. "Not quite. Look!" He pointed at a round spacecraft approaching rapidly.

"So what?" Chris said. "That's probably one of Monaal's craft come to guide us in."

Jerry peered at the silver-colored ship. "But we haven't notified Monaal, Chris. How would he know we're coming?"

"Oh, that's right," Chris said. "So who could it be?"

Steve sucked in his breath. "Guess!"

Chris groaned. "Oh, no! Not Cyclo!" Steve nodded.

The spaceship passed over the shuttle. There was no mistaking the J with a spear through it. Suddenly the shuttle began to vibrate violently. Smoke rose in thin wisps from the control panels. The pilots looked alarmed.

"All our controls have gone dead," one of them exclaimed.

Chris looked at them. "But you can make contact with the moon stations, can't you?"

The pilots shook their heads. "The communication system is out too," one of them said.

Chris looked anxiously out the window. "What do we do now?" he asked.

"Unless we can change our course," one pilot said, "we crash into the moon!"

CHAPTER 10

Jerry to the Rescue

It was quiet in the shuttle as the ship listed gently to one side. The moon grew larger and larger. The pilots pulled off the control-panel covering. They found many wires burned and some fused together.

One pilot frowned and shook his head. "The life-support system is out too."

Chris spoke up. "If we could let Monaal know where we are, he could send up a rescue ship, couldn't he?"

"I imagine so," one pilot said, "if we had a communication system that was operable."

Jerry watched quietly as the pilots worked. One of them sat back. "It's hopeless! We can't do anything with this mess!"

Jerry leaned forward. "Is the antenna intact?" he asked.

"Yes," a pilot said. "It's the system *inside* that's disabled."

Jerry looked at the integrated circuits, capacitors, and endless strands of undamaged wire that laced the control panel. "When I was a kid," he said, "I once made a crystal radio set, hooked it up to the gismo, and heard Monaal. When I added an old telephone, I was able to talk to him." He rubbed his chin. "Maybe I could rig up something like that now."

Chris looked surprised. "Out of all this junk?"

Jerry nodded. "I said *maybe*. Are there any pliers around here?"

A pilot handed him a pair.

Jerry began pulling out long strands of wire. He turned to Chris. "Give me that cardboard tube that contains the U.N. document of acceptance."

Chris did so.

Carefully Jerry wound the wires tightly around the tube. Chris looked puzzled. His grandfather said, "I'm making a primitive tuning coil." He turned to the pilots. "Where does the antenna lead into the control panel?"

A pilot showed him.

Jerry attached the end of the wire from the tuning coil to the antenna. "Next," he said, "I'll need a tuning bar. The needle from this airspeed indicator should do." He removed the needle, bent it slightly, and attached the wire to it. "Now, a diode, a capacitor, and your headset, sir, and we may have it."

A pilot handed Jerry a headphone with the attached mike. Then Jerry took the gismo from his wrist.

On one of the flat panel covers the pilots had removed from the console, Jerry laid out the circuit. He screwed down the tuning bar and attached the wire from the bar to the gismo. He cut the wires that held the headset to the console and attached one of them to the shuttle bulkhead. "This is to ground the mike to the shuttle skin," he explained. The other wire he attached to the gismo. "Now we'll hook up the capacitor to the gismo and see if we're in business."

He checked all the wire connections, put the headset on, and spoke into the mike. "Calling Monaal of Throal at Intergalactic Way Station, Natural Satellite, Planet Three, over." He grinned at the boys. "I still remember that."

There was a faint crackling from the headset. Jerry tried again.

On his third attempt, the gismo glowed cherry red, and Monaal's high-pitched voice came through. "This is Monaal of Throal speaking. Who is this?"

"An old friend of yours, Jerry Cole of Planet Earth."

"Jerry!" Monaal exclaimed. "Where *are* you?"

"Nearing the moon in a disabled shuttle craft. Our life-support system is out, and we're heading for a crash on the moon's surface. Can you help us out?"

"I'll send up a rescue craft at once!" Monaal said.

It was only a matter of minutes before two circular craft shot up from the moon and threw a gigantic net over the shuttle. They brought the disabled ship down into the way station crater on the far side of the moon.

Chris and Steve watched eagerly as the great hangar door slid open. A piloteer fastened a long cord to the shuttle and drew it inside.

Monaal and his daughter Kaali were waiting to greet them with handshakes and hugs, as Chris, Steve, and Jerry climbed down from the shuttle. The two pilots watched, round-eyed, as Gat leaped from the console platform and extended a long hairy arm to them, grinning from one big ear to the other.

In Monaal's office, Jerry, Chris, and Steve related their adventures while searching for the three hidden messages.

When they had finished, Monaal said, "You have all shown great courage and resourcefulness in completing this mission."

"One thing I'd like to know, Mr. Monaal," Chris said. "Did you know Cyclo was going to interfere this way?"

Monaal shook his head. "I had an idea he might object, but it didn't occur to me that he would hamper you."

"Poor being!" Jerry said. "If he would stop worrying about other planets, go back to Jovan, and stamp out his wars, he'd be much better off."

"You are right," Monaal said. "And it's the example of beings like you that may change his mind someday."

Jerry sighed. "Let's hope so!"

"But come," Monaal said. "We must now prepare to return to your United Nations of Earth with our delegation from the Intergalactic Federation."

The disabled shuttle was quickly repaired by mechanics at the way station. The shuttle pilots marveled at the advanced tools and machinery used.

As the shuttle sped toward Alpha City, Chris gazed out the window at the fleet of spacecraft that accompanied them. Gat, the hairy dwarf, and Brill, the willowy giant from Gamadrome, were among the delegates. Chris chuckled. "Hey, Steve, can you see Mr. Bryant's face when the news of this hits TV?"

"Yeah, won't he be surprised! And it should put us back in his good graces for what happened on the moon."

"Right. Now he'll understand why we couldn't explain everything." Suddenly Chris grinned at Steve. "Say, I know what. Let's take Gat and Brill with us to our next Scout meeting. That'll give Bryant the biggest surprise of all!"

www.ingramcontent.com/pod-product-compliance
Lightning Source LLC
Chambersburg PA
CBHW020136180626
46810CB00004B/1593